*"You believe a member of the society stole the. . . Could you explain what the notes are?"*

"The Washington notes are exactly what the name implies. They are notes that George Washington penned on a piece of leather. When he spent the night in the house."

I was glad she could not see my skeptical grin. "So George Washington slept there?"

"Oh yes. And ate at least two meals, possibly three. He planned his campaign from the first bedchamber. And that is why the house is so important."

"Where did the notes come from? And why would he write on leather?"

"They were written on a piece of leather most likely cut from the bottom of a chair."

"The father of our country vandalized furniture?"

Don't miss out on a single one of our great mysteries. Contact us at the following address for information on our newest releases and club information:

Heartsong Presents—MYSTERIES! Readers' Service
PO Box 721
Uhrichsville, OH 44683
Web site: www.heartsongmysteries.com

Or for faster action, call 1-740-922-7280.

# George Washington Stepped Here

## A Karen Maxwell Mystery

K. D. Hays

HEARTSONG
PRESENTS
MYSTERIES

This book is dedicated to Trent and Meg with all my love. (And in case you're wondering, I flipped a coin to determine who would be listed first.)

I'd like to thank my critique partners Lisa Cochrane, Christie Kelley, Kathy Love, Janet Mullany, and Kate Poole; my editors Susan Downs, Candice Speare, and Ellen Tarver; and also Sharon Zarate for sharing her expertise about the business of private investigation. I also owe thanks to my mom, Betty Dolan, and husband, Jim Weidman, for introducing me to some of the best mysteries ever written.

ISBN 978-1-59789-594-1

Cover design: Kirk DouPonce, DogEared Design
Cover illustration: Jody Williams

*Our mission is to publish and distribute inspirational products offering exceptional value and biblical encouragement to the masses.*

Printed in the U.S.A.

"I don't have time for this," Dave muttered as he picked up a chocolate chip cookie off my desk.

Setting down the box of new "DS Investigations" stationery that I had just picked up from the printer's, I reached over to snatch the remaining cookie out of his reach. "That makes two of us. I don't have time for you taking my lunch, either. And why are you sitting at my desk?"

He shrugged as he leaned back in the swivel chair. "Technically, it's my desk. I own the firm now, so I own everything in this office." A smile of satisfaction gradually spread over his face as he gazed around the shabby second-floor apartment of the old house that served as the headquarters for the newly renamed DS Investigations. Rays of afternoon sun shining through the drafty windows illuminated sprays of dust motes in the air, and I made a mental note to have another talk with the landlord about the cleaning service.

After hiding the cookie behind a plant, I picked up the box of stationery again and put it in a drawer. "You really are enjoying having the firm all to yourself now, aren't you?"

"Yes," he sighed with contentment. "Yes, I am." The chair groaned alarmingly as Dave turned and leaned farther back.

I reached behind him to grab a tray of invoices before they tipped onto the floor. Then I tried to make my next question sound casual. "Does that mean you've changed your mind about taking on a new partner?" I winced at the childish, hopeful sound in my voice. As much as I wanted Dave to let me try some of the real investigative work that had been handled by his former partner, I didn't want him to see how badly I wanted it. He was, after all, my younger brother. I had guilted him into giving me a job after my divorce, but now, if I wanted him to give me a better job, I was going to have to earn it.

He nodded slowly. "I think I'm ready to fly solo for a while."

"With a couple of stewardesses to clean up after you." I threw out an empty paper coffee cup and unfolded a wadded-up receipt he had left in my in-box.

He grinned sheepishly. "Well, yeah. I don't have time for that paper. . .stuff."

"You mean the paper stuff that enables you to draw a paycheck?"

"That's why I hired you and Brittany, sis."

I leaned back against the file cabinet. "Well, are you going to let me get back to work, or do you intend to handle the Nabco client report yourself?"

He launched himself forward out of the chair, gesturing for me to be seated as if he were a king bestowing favors on a loyal subject. "Oh no, I'll leave that to you."

As I sat, he leaned toward me and lowered his voice. "But I was wondering if you might like the chance to take on an investigative assignment."

Those were the words I'd been waiting to hear for the past five years—ever since I had started working for him. I'd filed papers and typed reports and copied files and done 90 percent of the work that kept the office functioning, but never had I had the chance to do the 10 percent of the work that kept the office alive. Investigation. Just the thought of getting out of the dank, dim old building—even if it was only to go into other often danker and dimmer buildings of Ellicott City—set my heartbeat up a notch.

But if I let him know this was the opportunity I'd been waiting for, he'd press his advantage over me somehow. So I tried to act as if I didn't really care one way or the other.

"I might be," I allowed.

"Are you doing anything on Saturday?"

My hopes plummeted as I waved toward the desk calendar. "I'm doing *everything* on Saturday. Evan has a game at nine o'clock, and then I believe he has team pictures at eleven, which should give me approximately fifteen minutes to drive Alicia to her drama class, which is at least twenty minutes away. If I don't hit any traffic lights."

"Is that all?" He grimaced with annoyance as he shoved the last bite of cookie into his mouth and licked a smear of chocolate off his fingers. Since he has no family of his own, he doesn't quite believe how much time kids take up. He thinks I spend my weekends soaking in the tub reading romance novels.

"Well, no." I brushed the cookie crumbs off my Rolodex. "Then I need to take the dog to the vet and get to the store to get something to organize Alicia's closet—oh, and a new rug for the bathroom floor—and then I have to get back in time to meet the termite inspector—"

He waved to cut me off. "But you can do that stuff another day, right?"

I hate it when he interrupts. "No."

Okay, that was not strictly true. Bathroom accessories would no doubt remain available for purchase in the days beyond Saturday. "When else am I going to have time to do this stuff?" I asked.

He nodded toward his office, an enclave of disorganized papers and empty sardine cans that was the only private space in the whole agency. Formerly occupied by the senior partner, Nate, the office had succumbed to Dave's slovenly influences before we'd even finished cleaning up from Nate's retirement party. "I have a job for you on Saturday."

"You promised I wouldn't have to work weekends." I hadn't said no, and he knew it. This was all part of the bargaining process. If he could, he'd get me to take this assignment for free to gain experience. I wasn't that desperate—or at least I didn't think I was.

"This is a special job—you might call it an undercover assignment."

"I don't care. I'm not working on a Saturday," I insisted, although at the same time I was trying to remember where to find the termite company's phone number so I could call to reschedule the inspection.

Dave assumed a singsong voice, as if trying to lure a child to an ice cream truck. "This is real investigative work."

I hesitated. He was going to call my bluff at any moment. "I still don't care."

He sighed and shrugged himself off the door frame. "Well, I guess I'll have to give the assignment to Brittany, then." He turned to go back into his office.

Uh-oh, I'd held out too long. "Doesn't she have finals or something?" I couldn't leave things this way. I couldn't let Dave give an assignment, a real undercover assignment, to a mere college student who mishandled phone messages and misspelled half the words on the reports she typed. "I wouldn't want to take valuable time away from her studies."

Dave turned back and pursed his lips. "She's majoring in criminal justice. Seems like the extra work would help in her studies."

"Are you paying overtime?"

"Comp time."

"Including transportation?"

Dave pursed his lips again, this time adding a twist to the side that gives the impression that he's pondering some deep philosophical question, which is a false impression because he doesn't have the depth of character to ponder any philosophical questions whatsoever. He had me and he knew it. "One way."

"Okay, I'll do it."

"Great. I'll get you the file." He shuffled back to his office while I contemplated my calendar with a sigh.

Back when Dave offered me work in his investigation agency, I had no illusions about what the job would be like. I would not be tracking down ruthless murderers or underworld jewel thieves. I would not mingle with the rich and famous, looking for clues in the midst of glamorous undercover liaisons. And I would not form an unlikely friendship with a rival police detective who hated my methods but grudgingly admired my results. That was TV. Instead, I would be answering phones, filing papers, and doing background checks on the computer. I could get my work finished in time to pick up the kids from school, help with homework, and get dinner ready before Cub Scouts. And in the first few years after the divorce, that was all I wanted.

But after a while, as my active anger toward my philandering ex-husband faded to a general sense of disgust, I found myself growing tired of the day-to-day sameness of my job. Maybe being a mom wasn't as much fun as it used to be. I could no longer just coast through the day, waiting anxiously to hug Alicia and Evan as they got off the school bus.

They had told me to stop hugging them at the bus stop, for one thing.

And there was no one else to wait for.

So the opportunity to maybe turn my job into a real career was one I simply could not pass up.

A few moments later Dave handed me a folder with a brown drink ring on the corner and the name McGregor scrawled on the front.

When I opened the folder, a lone sheet of scratch paper fluttered to the desk. I looked up at him in disgust. "This is it? Where's the case sheet? Where are the contact forms? Where's the log?"

He scratched his nose. "I figured you could do all that before you go out on Saturday."

"Go? Go where?" I picked up the piece of paper. "Seventeen seventy-six? Is it a hotel room?"

"It's a date, actually."

"Oh, great. Instead of a *where*, I get a *when*. So this is a time-travel assignment?"

He grinned. "Yeah, sort of."

"What's that supposed to mean?"

As he headed back toward his office, he beckoned for me to follow. "Look, I do have more information; I just haven't put it all together yet." He added in a low voice, "Because she keeps calling and interrupting me." As he sank into his chair, he pulled a yellow Post-it note off a box of crackers next to his computer monitor. "This is the client. Eileen McGregor."

I followed him into the room reluctantly, hoping the sour smell coming from the bookcase could be traced to something with a lid that might eventually be closed.

He rolled his chair over to me, holding out the adhesive-backed note like an angler trying to lure in a trout. "She's an old lady on the board of the Reisterstown Historical Society. Y' know, the 'hysterical society'? One of those types that wants to keep everything the way it looked in 'the old days.' Anyway, she says the society is missing a valuable artifact. Something having to do with George Washington."

"Has she filed a police report?"

"No."

"Why not?"

He shrugged. "My guess is because the item is worthless and she thinks the police won't do anything to help recover it. But I'm sure you'll find out. She's paid us a nine-hundred-dollar retainer, so I told her we'd start right away." He fished around in his shirt pocket. "Why don't you deposit this on your way home?" He handed me a folded check.

I sighed. "No deposit slip, no case number—you didn't even endorse it."

"You can sign my name as well as I do."

"Okay." I had pretty much given up on getting Dave to keep financial stuff in order. I just should have been grateful that the check wasn't lost or covered with mustard. I opened the nearly empty McGregor file and placed the check inside. "So what's with the date?"

He leaned over to squint at the paper. "I was wrong, actually. I mean, it is a date, but it's also a place. The 1776 House."

"The 1776 House? Never heard of it. Did Betsy Ross make flags there or something?"

Dave shrugged. "Maybe she knit the Declaration of Independence there. In any case, it's the place where they kept this missing artifact. Guess it's probably in Reisterstown somewhere."

I snapped the file shut. "You didn't even get an address?"

"I got a check. And I have the lady's phone number. I figured you or Brittany could manage the details."

"So what do you want me to do?"

He settled back in what I still thought of as Nate's big leather chair. "You said you had the kids this weekend, right? Well, take them up there and pretend you're a mother bringing her kids to learn about history. And then you can ask around—"

"Wait a minute!" I planted my hands on my hips as I glared at him. "I *am* a mother. And I *do* try to take my kids to learn about history. Maybe not as often as—"

He held up his hands as if fending off physical blows from me. "What are you so upset about?"

"This is not an undercover assignment!" I smacked the file against the palm of my hand. "You said it would be an undercover assignment. A soccer mom going undercover as a soccer mom is not much of a challenge!"

"Yes, that's the whole point. You'll be convincing."

"I'll be bored stiff."

He shrugged. "Then you'll be convincingly bored."

"Dave! This is not how I want to spend my Saturdays."

"You're getting paid. Besides, it's just one Saturday."

I sighed. "Okay. I guess you're right."

But he wasn't. For that matter, neither was I.

$$\sim$$

I didn't think that Betsy Ross ever lived in Reisterstown, but other than that, I couldn't really say anything for certain about this 1776 House. So the next day I called Mrs. McGregor for some background, including the address of the site, since the only address I had was the one on her personal check.

"Good morning. This is Karen Maxwell of DS Investigations."

"Wait while I fix the volume," a woman's voice ordered sternly.

*Wham!*

I surmised that either she dropped the phone or a large object just flattened her house. Various muffled scraping sounds followed before the imperious voice returned. "Hello?" she asked.

"Is this Mrs. McGregor?"

"Yes."

"I am Karen Maxwell with DS Investigations. I have

a few questions to ask, but I will try not to take up too much of your—"

"Well," she huffed, "I don't think I have ever talked to you before."

"No, ma'am. You spoke with my brother, Dave Sarkesian. I need to get some information from you about the case before I—"

"I thought he was handling the case. He told me he would see to it personally."

I could almost *hear* her pout through untold miles of fiber-optic phone line.

"This is a matter of some delicacy, you understand," she continued, "and I do not want it bandied about all over town. That is why I called Mr. Sarkesian instead of the police."

"I understand, ma'am. Can I get the address of the—"

Her tone grew even haughtier. "Well, I really thought I'd be working with Mr. Sarkesian himself. I'm not sure I should be giving confidential information to *you*."

So I wasn't good enough for her. Fine. Then I would just have to pretend to be Dave, in a way. I put a simpering smile onto my face, hoping the expression would come through in my voice. "Mrs. McGregor, I am Mr. Sarkesian's *secretary*. I am simply trying to collect information so that *he* can devote his mental energy to the science of investigation."

"Oh. In that case, what do you need to know?"

I took down the address of the site and contact information, and she even offered bank account information to authorize monthly withdrawals from her account should the investigation expenses exceed the initial retainer fee. This woman was serious about finding the missing—

The missing thing. Whatever it was. That was what I had to find out next.

"Now, ma'am, I need information about the missing artifact."

"Won't Mr. Sarkesian come to discuss the matter in person?"

*Not likely.* I think he had already dismissed this one as an open-and-shut case, meaning that she had opened her checkbook and he had shut his wallet with the check inside.

But I came up with an answer for her. "He prefers to be briefed in advance of a meeting so that he has adequate time to think."

"Oh."

"So what can you tell me about the missing artifact?"

"Well, no one knows how the thief got it out of the glass case, because only two of us have the key, you know, and I would never steal it, of course, and neither would Ann." Her words came faster and faster as if she were afraid she would forget a detail. "Ann Bleckenstrauss is the chair of the Exhibits Committee, so this year she has the other key. But she did say she thought we should have an extra copy—of course she also thought we should donate everything to the Daughters of the American Patriots for safekeeping, although I thought if we just put an electronic sensor on the case. . . But when the board discussed the motion, they—although Jimmy Reynolds might have persuaded them to put a sensor on the case if he hadn't been out for hip surgery that week—"

"What case are you referring to?" Yes, it was rude to interrupt the client, but her zealous rant was already driving me crazy. I had a pretty good idea of why Dave had given this assignment to me.

"The permanent exhibits case," she said pointedly, as if I were a fool not to have already known this. "Well, Ann has keys to all the exhibit cases—"

"But what was *in* the exhibits case? What was stolen?"

"The Washington notes!" The pitch of her voice rose to an almost painful level. "The Washington notes were taken right from our own locked permanent exhibits case. And that is why I believe it was someone within the society."

"You believe a member of the society stole the. . . Could you explain what the notes are?"

"The Washington notes are exactly what the name implies. They are notes that George Washington penned on a piece of leather. When he spent the night in the house."

I was glad she could not see my skeptical grin. "So George Washington slept there?"

"Oh yes. And ate at least two meals, possibly three. He planned his campaign from the first bedchamber. And that is why the house is so important."

"Where did the notes come from? And why would he write on leather?"

"They were written on a piece of leather most likely cut from the bottom of a chair."

"The father of our country vandalized furniture?"

In the pause that followed, I could just about

hear her glare at me for impugning the name of the great man. "It was wartime," she said finally. "He did what he had to do. Now, the notes were found during renovations during the 1920s. They prove Washington's connection to the house. Without the notes, the house is simply another old building." The pitch of her voice had returned to normal levels, but she now sounded as if she were choking back tears. "We must have them back. And no one must know that they're missing, or we will be certain to suffer a reduction in visitors. Everyone comes to see the Washington notes."

I tapped my pen on my notepad. "If the notes are so important to the house, why would someone within the society take them away?"

"There are those members of the board"—she sniffed in derision—"who believe the notes to be fake. They have insisted that we should remove them from display until they can be authenticated. The rest of the board, of course, votes this proposal down every year. But I think she has grown so desperate that she would forcibly remove the notes rather than admit they're wrong."

"She?"

Her voice dropped to a bitter sneer. "Paula Lowell."

I took down the name. "So you think Paula Lowell stole the piece of leather."

"The Washington notes."

I cringed. "Er, yeah, the notes. Or at least you're confident they were stolen by someone in the organization?"

"Paula Lowell is a member of the board, as is her sister, Patty. And we cannot deny that she serves with great dedication. But she does not trust any historical fact unless she herself has discovered it. So her dedication is really most trying." She sighed. "I can only hope that someday she and her sister will find a site more to their liking."

"Do you think if she finds a new site she'll return the piece of—the Washington notes? If she took them?"

Her voice grew strident again. "I am not willing to wait for her to decide on a proper time to return them. I want the notes back in their case straightaway. That is why we hired your brother. At the end of next month, the society will finally have the chance to host a visit from Lucinda Fotheringill, president of the Daughters of the American Patriots. We must have the notes back in place by then, or the 1776 House will be deemed a sham, an unimportant relic."

I was certain now why my brother assigned this "case" to me. The woman sounded nuts. And it sounded as if she worked with people who were equally, if not more, insane. Stealing an old piece of leather. Who would go to such lengths? And why would this woman pay nine hundred dollars to get it back? Dave handed all this craziness to me while he went on to work with more appealing clients.

Before I left that afternoon, I briefed Dave on the conversation.

"You're doing great." He layered two anchovies on a cracker and tipped the whole mess into his mouth. "Uf oo oo a oo ob, ah an et oo av or ases."

"Can we try that again? I'm not very fluent in cracker."

He swallowed. "If you do a good job with this, I

can let you have more cases. Take the lead on them."

"Great." I didn't know whether to believe him. But regardless, I still had to take care of the administrative work, or none of us would have any cases. I dropped a file onto his desk. "You need to sign these, put them in the attached envelopes, and drop them in the mailbox before you leave."

"Sign, envelopes, mailbox. Got it."

"See you!" I put on my sunglasses and started for the door.

He opened the folder. "Oh yeah. Hey, thanks for taking that 'hysterical society' lady off my hands. I've got enough to do with the Petrinelli case."

"You mean you'd rather spend your time trailing the very attractive Mrs. Petrinelli rather than listening to poor old Mrs. McGregor."

He grinned. "You'll have a great time with the kids tomorrow. The old lady told me all about the house and lovely garden. They even demonstrate how to cook over an open fire. I'm sure you'll pick up some great tips for the kitchen."

I narrowed my eyes at him, not that he could see with the sunglasses I was wearing. "You owe me, buddy."

"Just think of this as a test, Karen."

"And you the teacher. Now that is scary." But I smiled as I walked out. For all his obnoxious behavior, my brother is a fairly successful investigator, probably because he has a remarkable ability to understand what motivates people. Me, for instance. Just the promise of more interesting work was enough to induce me to give up a weekend afternoon. I knew I could do a good job with this case. In one visit, I would find the thief and get her to confess and cough up the piece of ratty leather before the weekend was out.

All I had to do was convince my kids to go along with it.

## 2

As I plowed through the loose gravel in the parking lot of the 1776 House, I looked over at Evan and realized we had a problem. "Leave the soccer ball in the van!"

"But, Mom, the coach said he wanted us to practice every spare minute." Evan clutched the ball to his chest.

"Well, you're not going to have any spare minutes for a while. We'll be touring the house."

"I can practice dribbling while I listen. See?" He demonstrated by kicking the ball around me in a tight circle.

"Put the ball back."

He continued in a second orbit around Planet Mom.

I reached for the ball with my foot and missed by an embarrassingly large margin. "Where is your sister?" I scanned the parking lot, the gardens, and the entrance to the gift shop. Then I saw that she was still reading in the back of the van. I banged on the window. "Come on. We're waiting for you. Evan, put the ball inside."

He started around me again, this time with a big grin on his face. As Alicia opened the sliding door, I stepped in front of Evan, scooped up the ball, and tossed it inside.

"Ouch!"

Alicia's grunt was more one of indignation than pain, so if I had hit her with the ball, it wasn't too serious.

"Sorry." I offered her a halfhearted, this-is-what-you-get-for-ignoring-your-mom smile. "Don't forget to shut the door when you get out."

She eased herself out, gave me a nasty look, and re-opened her folio of drama scripts, reading as she walked slowly toward the entrance to the house.

I turned to Evan. "Come on. This visit won't take too long, and then you can practice afterwards." As I looked at him, I felt a frown aging my forehead yet again. "Did you have that chocolate mustache when they took the team picture?" I always send the fall soccer pictures to relatives, and I didn't want them thinking Evan had grown premature facial hair.

He squinted as if trying to look through the inside of his face. "We had chocolate granola bars after the game."

I sighed, pulled a tissue from my purse, and handed it to him. "I think you'll find it tastes much better if you get it *in* your mouth next time."

He grinned sheepishly. "Okay."

Alicia's shuffling footsteps drew her up to the gift shop entrance at the end of the building. She reached for the doorknob, no doubt drawn by an instinctive adolescent need to spend money.

"No, Alicia. The entrance is over here." I pointed to the front door of the two-story house that was smaller than I'd expected. It looked pretty much like an ordinary house, except that it was built of brick that seemed as if it might crumble to powder if you looked at it wrong.

As we climbed the worn marble steps, Evan read the small sign framed on the door. "Please enter through the gift shop." He turned around, jumped down the steps, and nearly flattened his sister, who was still immersed in her book of plays.

"Evan, please step next to people rather than on top of them. Alicia, put the book away. I want you to pay attention during the tour."

Alicia rolled her eyes but tucked the book into her shoulder bag without verbal complaint. My struggle with preteen rebellion was still in the early stages, thankfully.

As we stepped into a long narrow gift shop crowded with shelves of painted porcelain, lace-edged tea towels, and a host of other things I couldn't imagine anyone wanting, the cloying smell of too many different varieties of scented candles assaulted our noses. We were greeted by an older woman standing behind the counter and dressed in colonial attire. "Welcome to the 1776 House, young sir and good ladies. Have you visited us before?" As she spoke, she bobbed her head, fluttering the oversized ruffles on her white cap.

I shook my head. "No, no, this is our first visit. Evan, put down the pen."

"But, Mom, look! It's shaped like a gun."

The lady behind the counter smiled. "That is a musket, young man. See if you can spot one just like it in the museum."

"You brought us to a museum?" He pointed the tiny weapon/writing implement at me accusingly. "I thought you said we were just going to look at a house for a few minutes."

"It's a house-museum," I admitted.

Alicia had already found a refrigerator case somewhere, because she planted a plastic bottle of orange soda on the counter. "How much?"

"It's one dollar and twenty-five cents." The lady at the counter laid a hand on top of the bottle. "But you cannot take this into the house."

Alicia wrapped her hand possessively around the soda.

I put on my best bargaining smile. "After the tour, Alicia."

Her hand lingered on the bottle just long enough to show her utter contempt for the rules. Then she returned the soda to the small glass-doored refrigerator in the back of the shop.

I glanced at the shelves of blue-and-white pottery, crocheted doilies, iron trivets, and perfumed soaps, hoping they made most of their money from the souvenirs rather than the admission fees, because I forgot to stop at the ATM. "How much is the tour?"

"The tour is free, *with* museum admission. One adult, two students—that's nine dollars."

I handed her a ten. "I need a receipt. Rats."

"Excuse me?" The lady behind the counter frowned so severely that the blue ribbons on her cap drooped to match.

I grinned apologetically. "Er, no, I was talking to my daughter. Alicia, remind me to write down the mileage before we leave. I forgot to get it earlier." I reached out to take the receipt from the frowning lady.

"Why do you need the mileage?" Alicia asked.

I waved for her to be quiet. "I'll tell you later."

A short woman—also dressed like Betsy Ross— sailed into the room, the ruffles on her cap waving smartly in the wind she created with her own rapid progress. "Are you good people ready to begin the tour?"

I started to answer affirmatively but then closed my mouth and simply nodded instead so she wouldn't recognize my voice. The tour guide's name tag said EILEEN MCGREGOR. I didn't want her, or anyone else in the house, to know I was there to investigate, at least not yet.

"Very well." She adjusted the volume on her hearing aid. "We will begin our tour in the hall. Please follow me up the stairs, and as we go on our way, we ask that you not touch any of the exhibits, but you may take any pictures you like. Except for the ones on the walls, of course."

My son snickered. Naturally, he reached out to the first painting we passed, and I slapped his hand away with the alacrity learned from my fourth-grade teacher at St. Bernadette's.

The room the guide referred to as a hall was really more of a general all-purpose room, as far as I could see. It had a sofa, a table set up with food, and a four-poster bed in one corner, like an efficiency apartment.

"This was the home of Josiah Barnswallow from 1757 until 1793," Mrs. McGregor announced in an unnecessarily loud voice. "He was a merchant and a great patriot who supported the colonial army with supplies and even his own service in the Maryland militia. He served as an aide to General George Washington and was a personal friend of the great man, as well. And there's more to that tale to come."

A cough sounded from the next room. I could hear footsteps but couldn't see anyone.

"Why does he have a bed in his hallway?" Evan asked.

I was pleased that he asked, since I wondered the same thing myself but had not yet figured out how to ask questions without using my voice.

Mrs. McGregor favored him with a displeased schoolteacher expression. "This room, young man, is not a hallway but a hall. The hall is the main living room in the house. Now, we have furnished the house to the year 1776, and by that time, Mr. Barnswallow had built a separate kitchen building out behind the house. But originally, all the cooking would have been done at that fireplace there."

"Did he cook from his bed? Why didn't he call this 'the bedroom'?" Evan asked.

She peered down her nose at him. "Mr. Barnswallow had fourteen children. There are beds in every room of the house."

While I looked around to see if I could spot the person who had coughed in the next room, Mrs. McGregor described the fabric of the bed curtains, pointed out the intricate carving on the legs of the bed and table, and discussed the vernacular style of the chairs around the table and the evidence of the influence of various furniture makers on design elements throughout the room.

Evan let out a fake snore.

I elbowed him in the ribs.

I did not see a glass case anywhere in the room, but I didn't expect to, since the missing artifact had been taken from a bedroom, and this was called the hall.

Even though it had a bed.

We were next shown through the parlor, while our guide lavished the same loving attention on furniture design.

"Notice the beautiful faux wood finish on the doors."

"Faux wood?" Alicia's face wrinkled in puzzlement. "But then what are the doors really made of?"

"Wood," Mrs. McGregor replied as she started briskly for the stairs. "But fake wood was more fashionable than real wood."

The coughing sounded again, and another costumed woman appeared in the doorway of the room we had just vacated. Her frowning face was crowned by a big black hat that accentuated her pointed nose and chin. "Ahem." She cast a withering look of disgust at our tour guide before turning to address her remarks to us. "The door was painted to resemble a more expensive, imported wood. It was the *variety and grade* of wood used in public rooms that demonstrated status." As she and Mrs. McGregor glared at each other in a brief moment of mutual antipathy, I wondered if I might possibly be seeing Paula Lowell. But she turned and walked out a door that led to the yard in back before I could think up a reasonable question to keep her in the room.

Mrs. McGregor fumed as if she'd just watched a pesky mouse disappear into a hole and knew it was now futile to make any attempt to catch it.

We shuffled upstairs and visited the nursery and the green bedchamber. There was then only one room left, and I was ready to run over our guide in my haste to see it so we could get out of the house before I fell asleep on my feet or my son succeeded in touching one of the ugly portraits, which would no doubt set off an alarm monitored by the the Hysterical Society Touching Police.

"And now, the 1776 House is pleased to present the first bedchamber. During August of 1777, General George Washington slept in this room while en route to Philadelphia. He and his aides, including Mr. Barnswallow, of course, planned much of their strategy for the upcoming Battle of the Brandywine right here in this room." With a dramatic flourish, Mrs. McGregor stepped aside to let us enter.

Alicia peered inside but did not actually commit to taking a full step.

Evan walked in, looked at each wall, and turned around to march back out. "Can we go now? We've had enough history for today."

"No, we haven't," I whispered hoarsely. This was the room I needed to examine. I took mental inventory of the red, white, and blue striped bed curtains, the chest of drawers with a washbowl and pitcher, the painting of Washington hanging over the fireplace (out of Evan's reach, fortunately), and the trunk propped open to display what appeared to be George Washington's full dress uniform. Nowhere did I see a glass case of any kind, empty or full.

Mrs. McGregor moved to the door. "Thank you for visiting the 1776 House. You are invited to tour the grounds on your own and meet the. . ." Her face fell into a sneer. "The *actors* in the kitchen, blacksmith shop, and springhouse."

I almost stopped her and told her who I was and of my need to explore the room in more detail. But I didn't. This was my only chance to look around as an ordinary visitor. Other people who worked here might reveal something if I asked the right questions and if they thought I was just another tourist.

I could come back to examine this room later.

Mrs. McGregor led us back downstairs to the parlor and pointed to a doorway that appeared to lead into the gift shop. "We hope you will have time to visit our store before you leave. This house receives no federal or state funding and is entirely dependent upon the support of the community to remain open."

"I'm going to support the house, Mom." Alicia started toward the gift shop.

"Will you buy me one, too?" Evan pleaded. "I promise I'll pay you back from my next week's allowance."

I handed him a five. "You already owe her your next two weeks' allowance. But I'll buy you each a soda if you won't complain while we visit the outbuildings."

"Do we have to?" Evan whined.

"Do you have to what?" I asked. "Complain?"

"No." He kicked the toe of his shoe against the dark floorboards. "Do we have to look at any more boring stuff?"

"Yes." I patted the money in his hand. "Get a drink. I'll meet you outside."

I was not bringing the kids with me again on an assignment. Ever.

While they sought the comforts of the refrigerated beverage case, I stepped out the back door that led directly into the yard, the door used earlier by the black-hatted woman I hoped was Paula Lowell.

The yard turned out to be a small expanse of packed dirt with sporadic tufts of grass and a small square garden enclosed by a low fence made of uneven sticks. Three outbuildings, two made of brick and one made of squared-off logs, stood at the back of the lot.

I decided I had the best chance of finding Paula Lowell in the kitchen that Mrs. McGregor had mentioned, so I started for the building with the most smoke pouring from the stone chimney. But unless dinner had gone horribly awry, I realized from the odd smell that met me at the doorway that this building was not the kitchen. A tall, muscular man stood with his back toward me, pumping the handle of a giant fireplace bellows. Each blast of air sent sparks shooting toward the ceiling. Stepping away from the giant bellows, he pulled a glowing red bar from the flames. He pounded the bar with an iron hammer, the ripple of muscles just barely visible through the thin white shirt. It was a shirt with puffy sleeves, like the blouses we wore to school with our plaid jumpers.

But even with his long dark hair tied back in a ponytail, the blacksmith looked more like a pirate than a schoolgirl. A nice pirate. His frank, open features and bright blue eyes made him look too earnest to be dangerous, despite his obvious physical strength.

He plunged the red-hot iron into a trough of cool water, sending up a hiss of steam. Then he looked up at me with a frown. "Why are ye dressed so strangely?"

## 3

M—me?" I looked down at my jeans. "I'm not."
Okay, so in his world, the pirate shirt was normal
and my jeans and sweater were "strange." I smiled and
decided to play along. "Why, this is the latest fashion."

He shook his head. "Must be the French. They
can be blamed for most of the fashion atrocities." He
pulled the iron out of the water and examined it for a
moment.

"What are you making?"

"It's a lantern hook. That is, it will be in a few
minutes." He laid the iron back in the fire and pumped
the bellows again.

I tried to think of some way to ask him about the
missing artifact. "Is that George Washington's horse-
shoe?" I pointed to a wall display hung with various
iron implements.

A look of pain flashed over his features. "I'm afraid
not."

"I heard that you had something of Washington's
here, but I didn't see anything in the house. . . ." I
hoped he would pick up the thread.

He removed the iron from the fire and placed it
in a vise. "I believe you'll find a good collection of
Washington artifacts at Mount Vernon."

"But you do have something of Washington's here,
don't you?"

He bent the iron to a ninety-degree angle, reposi-
tioned it in the vise, and bent it in another place. The

rigid iron moved like a pipe cleaner under his guidance. When the red glow began to fade, he set the piece back in the fire and began to pump the bellows once again.

I assumed he hadn't heard my question. "Do you have something of Washington's here?"

He looked at me for a moment, his blue eyes darkening with intensity as if trying to convey something he did not wish to put into words. After casting a glance at the doorway, he answered me in a low voice. "There is little real evidence connecting this house with Washington. We had a piece of writing rumored to have been inscribed by him, but they've removed it from public display until it's been authenticated. And it probably never will be, so it's just as well that it's gone. But it's a treasured story to many of the ladies in the house—that George Washington slept here, etc., etc.—so I hate to see them disappointed."

"You don't believe Washington slept here?"

He shook his head. "Of course, it's possible that George Washington *stepped* through here sometime. This road was a major trade route, and Mr. Barnswallow held a license to run a tavern. But there is no indication in any of Washington's diaries or other records that he spent any time here. This site is valuable for what it really is, an example of a typical home and business of the middling class. Most of us feel we do the public a disservice by repeating the old George Washington story, and we've been trying to remove all that nonsense from the house."

He moved with such grace and spoke with such quiet assurance that I found myself wishing I could simply continue watching and listening to him for the rest of the afternoon.

But I had a job to do. Who were the "us" who wanted to "remove" the Washington "nonsense" from the house? This man could give me a list of suspects if I could keep him talking. "Our tour guide seemed pretty proud that George Washington slept here," I observed casually. "So who *doesn't* believe that he did?"

He sighed, and then his mouth clamped into a thin line. Apparently asking directly for the information I wanted had been a bad idea.

"I'm just curious," I added quickly, to make it seem like no big deal.

"It's a matter that is frequently discussed at board meetings. First Thursday of every month. We're always looking for new volunteers."

And he wasn't going to discuss it now. He had turned away from me to examine a selection of metal rods in the back corner. Was he really busy, or was he trying to discourage my line of questioning?

"Oh, here you are." Evan sauntered in clutching a half-filled bottle of root beer. "The other building has a weird scary lady in it." He waved toward the blacksmith. "What's he doing?"

"Welcome to the smithy! You must be my new apprentice." The blacksmith had turned around again with a big welcoming smile, as if the arrival of Evan was what he had waited for all day. His eyes twinkled at the sight of Evan's discomfiture. "Don't just stand there, now," he admonished. "Step forward so I can show you your duties."

Evan looked at me uncertainly.

I plucked the soda bottle out of his hands. "Go on;

you heard the man. It's time for you to get to work."

And that gave me time to watch, just as I'd wanted.

⟡

After several very peaceful minutes in which the only sounds were Evan's voice as he asked questions, the gentle, low voice of the blacksmith as he answered, the creak of the bellows, and the clang of iron against the anvil, the tranquility was shattered by the arrival of a troop of Tiger Scouts.

"Ugh. First graders." Evan dropped the pliers he was holding and began to step away.

"Say thank you," I whispered.

He grabbed the soda from my hand. "Thank you," he called over his shoulder.

"You are most welcome. Come visit us again. We're here every Saturday." The blacksmith flashed that warm smile again, and I somehow felt as if it were my insides, rather than the bars of iron, that were melting in the heat.

And that meant, of course, that he would be married. No use even giving the man another thought.

We found Alicia sitting out in the yard, chewing a piece of grass and reading her plays.

I felt my nose wrinkle in disgust. "Aren't you afraid some animal stepped on that? Or worse?"

She shrugged.

I looked around the yard. Butterflies darted around sprays of goldenrod in the enclosed garden. "Do you want to visit the springhouse or the kitchen next?"

Evan took a swig of his root beer. "Which one is most likely to have a PS II?"

I laughed. "Since they didn't even have PlayStation I that long ago, that's a silly question."

"So was yours." He crossed his arms in front of his chest. "We've had enough of this, and we want to go home. Dad never makes us go to boring places like this on the weekends."

"Ten more minutes. You can last that long."

He rolled his eyes, expressing serious doubt that he would indeed survive the additional ten minutes without his video games.

"You had fun in there." I nodded toward the blacksmith shop.

"Yeah, but the scary lady is in *there*." He pointed toward a brick building that must be the kitchen, unless they kept a fire burning in the springhouse.

"What's so scary about her? I want to see." I pulled him toward the kitchen building. "Come with us, Alicia."

She hoisted herself up as if preparing for her own execution and trying to be a good sport about it.

"Now, I really think you will find this interesting," I continued as we climbed the brick step up into the kitchen, "because—"

"Restrain your loose tongue, if you please!" a woman barked at me as we entered the smoky room. "I've much to do to prepare the master's dinner and no time for idle distraction."

I flashed Evan a look but dared not say anything. This must be the "scary lady." Although she wore a flat white cap instead of a pointy hat, much of the rest of her appearance left a very witchlike impression. She wore multiple skirts, an apron, and a jacket of completely mismatched designs, with striped witch socks and ugly black shoes. Her thin face and long nose added to the witch impression. She minced something with quick strokes of a long, heavy knife, set down the implement, and swept the bits from the chopping board into a ceramic bowl. Then she turned to the fire and muttered to herself as she stirred the kettle hanging over the blaze.

I mustered the courage to speak. "What kind of brew—I mean stew—are you making?"

"Stew? What's a stew, pray tell? This is a ragout of beef and turnips."

Evan nudged me. "I think you were right," he whispered. "It is a brew."

The witch woman pointed at two iron kettles with coals stacked on the lids. "I've roasted venison and a pigeon pie. And now I must finish the blackberry fool. The master likes to dine late, at four of the clock, so thankfully I have more time than most cooks."

She told us more about her work in the kitchen and her life, or her character's life. I was ready to leave after about two minutes, because this woman plainly was not going to break character to answer my questions about George Washington.

But Alicia was fascinated. "She seems so. . .so real," she murmured.

So we stayed.

After listening to a lengthy discourse on the medicinal use of rosemary, I heard the sound of footsteps outside and turned toward the door, expecting to be run over by Tiger Scouts again.

But it was the blacksmith.

He bowed. "At your service. Good ladies, have you seen Mr. Holbrock about? I've finished with the lantern hook he commissioned from me."

I thought this break in the cook's kitchen monologue would be a good time to make our exit. Evan took the hint immediately; Alicia needed a little more coaxing. I smiled and nodded a farewell to the blacksmith and the cook, but I didn't say anything as I turned away because I didn't want to interrupt their conversation.

Although their voices dropped low, I could still hear them as I walked out. So I lingered to listen outside the door.

"Just be sure," the cook whispered in a low voice, "that he pays you in cash. Don't take anything in trade."

The blacksmith sighed. "I won't. But I don't think we have anything to worry about. I believe he learned his lesson. We can trust him."

"Ha!" the woman scoffed. "You're a more trusting soul than I am. Just don't take anything in trade. You don't want to end up holding stolen merchandise."

"I won't. Well, I've got to head out now. I'll see you next week."

"Please take some of this beef with you. And some pie."

"I don't need—"

Her voice softened. "Yes, you do need it, Brian. I know you don't have time to cook for yourself, with all those meetings."

"Well, all right. If you insist."

"I do."

Evan pulled at my sleeve. "Mom, I thought we were leaving."

I started away from the door with a guilty jerk. Ah, but there was no use feeling guilty for eavesdropping. That's what the job was all about.

We walked around the side of the house and headed toward the car, all of us silent, except for Evan banging his empty root beer bottle rhythmically against his leg. I reviewed what I had learned.

His name was Brian and he lived alone.

No, that was not why I had driven all the way out here, wasted an entire afternoon, and eavesdropped on private conversations. I did it because I was working.

I learned that someone, a Mr. Holbrock, had a reputation for pawning off stolen merchandise. I learned that Paula Lowell was not the only person pleased to see the Washington notes disappear. And I learned that the disappearance might be a secret even to the volunteers.

Okay, so I hadn't ferreted out the thief on my first day. I wasn't even certain I had identified Paula Lowell. But I did put in enough hours to use up part of the retainer. I would just have to come back on another Saturday.

As a volunteer.

Then I could ask all kinds of nosy questions and chalk it up to curiosity.

As long as I didn't have to wear witch clothes and a goofy cap.

## 4

"Why does it smell like burned toast in here?" Evan's nose wrinkled into an ugly expression that made him look far too much like a teenager. But he's only nine. So as he sat down to breakfast, I reached out to ruffle his already-mussed brown hair.

"I'm trying out a new air freshener." I pretended to hold up a bottle. "'Toaster oven crumbs.' Do you like it?"

He favored me with a sour look, and one eyebrow rose briefly before his whole face exploded into a yawn. It was plainly too early on a Monday morning to trifle with his sense of humor. "Where's the cereal?"

"I'm making scrambled eggs this morning." I poured the beaten eggs into a heated pan and nodded toward the bowl of apple slices, orange wedges, and diced pineapple. "Have some fruit while you're waiting."

"Ooh, pineapple!"

"Use a spoon." Even though I was facing the stove, I knew Evan was picking pieces of pineapple out with his fingers.

"Alicia," I called toward the stairs. "Breakfast is almost ready."

I listened for an answering moan or some other sign of life. When I heard a drawer slam upstairs, I felt fairly certain that she was up. The dog might have learned to open drawers to look for leftover crackers or candy in the kids' pockets, but she would have no incentive to *close* a drawer.

Apparently Evan never found much incentive to close drawers, either. Every time I entered his room, I fully expected the dresser to collapse forward on top of me from the combined weight of all the open drawers. He maintained this delicate balance of nature by storing most of his clothing on the floor.

The dirty clothing as well as the clean.

"That shirt has mustard on it." I pointed to a stain on his sleeve as I set the saltshaker on the table.

His face wrinkled in thought for a moment. "I have art first thing. I can pretend it's yellow paint."

"Or you could pretend you put on a clean shirt the first time. Go on up and change."

He slithered out of his chair and onto the floor, bearing a striking resemblance to the eggs I had poured into the pan a minute before. "I can't go to school, Mom. All my bones have evaporated."

"Very convincing." I nodded. "And you'd better get up before Alicia sees what a good actor you've become. She'll make you try out for community theater."

Evan jumped up with such speed he might have made it to the second floor without the use of the stairs.

"Watch where you're going, twerp!" Alicia's dulcet big-sisterly tones projected down from above.

"Sorry!" Evan actually sounded almost apologetic. His mood had apparently improved.

Alicia's, however, still needed work. She stalked into the kitchen with a disdainful frown, as if she were queen and I the court ambassador of a conquered nation that failed to pay sufficient tribute. "I don't have any clean socks."

"In the basket." I nodded toward a basket of socks and underwear on the floor. "They needed a little more time in the dryer this morning."

She sniffed, flipping a shock of ash blond hair out of her eyes. "You cooked breakfast?"

"Yes." I smiled as I scooped egg onto a plate and handed it to her.

For a moment she just looked at it as if not quite sure what to do.

"Sit down. I'll have your toast in a minute. I burned the first batch."

She shuffled over to the table wearing big furry slippers with perky ears and grinning faces that seemed a great deal more alert than she was. Orange juice sloshed over onto the table as she dropped her plate into place. "Do you have the day off work? You never have time to cook us breakfast on school days."

"I got up early today." I examined her feet for a moment. The slippers were miniature dogs that looked very much like our first pet, Molly. "Those are my slippers, aren't they?"

"You never wear them."

"It never seemed right somehow. I felt like I was banging poor Molly's head into the risers whenever I went up the stairs."

Alicia slurped her orange juice. "Did you see that dog on Saturday? It reminded me so much of Molly."

"A dog?" Evan asked as he landed back at the table. "Where?" He was wearing a dark-colored shirt, so if it wasn't actually clean, at least any stains would be less noticeable.

Alicia reached to take the piece of toast I handed

her. "At that house we went to. With the actors."

"Oh, the old house with the scary lady. Maybe she turned herself into a dog." Evan bared his teeth as if he planned to eat the toast I offered him right from my hand.

I shook my head.

He closed his mouth reluctantly and took the slice of toast in his hand.

"Did you see the dog, Mom?" Alicia persisted.

"No." I smiled. "But I'll look for it next time."

Evan's hand froze halfway to his mouth. "Next time?"

I hadn't planned to say anything about the 1776 House for a while, but since Alicia had already introduced the topic, I decided to forge ahead. "I think I might go back and volunteer at the site once in a while. I found it a very interesting place."

Evan dropped his toast. "Are you kidding?"

"It was kinda neat," Alicia mused as she attempted to spear a chunk of apple with her fork. "Not the tour part, but the cooking part." The apple skittered off her plate, launched across the place mat, and clung to the side of her juice glass.

I didn't bother to ask what Evan thought. Maybe I could find a soccer camp to send him to on Saturdays for the next few weeks. And this Saturday, both kids would be with their dad.

I paused for a moment, bracing myself for the usual burst of impotent rage that usually followed my thoughts about my ex and how he'd ruined our lives.

Maybe it was just the really good coffee I had made that morning, but the thought of Jeff bothered me hardly at all this time. I kissed Evan on the top of his head in a vain attempt to flatten an unruly tuft of hair.

"What was that for?" he asked as he wiped his mouth on a wadded-up napkin.

"Just because." I glanced at the clock. "Alicia, you'd better hurry up. Your bus will be here soon."

She shoveled the last bite of egg into her mouth, her eyes on the clock.

"Don't forget to brush your teeth," I called as she dashed away from the table.

It seemed that nothing could defeat my good mood. Even the wail of the garbage truck as it crushed trash down the street and lumbered forward to collect the garbage that probably hadn't been put out yet failed to lower my spirits. "Evan, did you remember to take out the trash?"

His face froze in a guilty expression. "No." He started to get up.

"Never mind. I'll get it." I rushed to the sliding glass door that led out back, then ran across the uneven deck planking, down the short flight of steps, and through the mud to where the trash can was propped against the side of the house. Fumbling with the gate latch, I got the can through and down to the curb just as the garbage truck squealed to a stop in front of me.

"Hello," my neighbor called cheerfully from across the street, yelling to compensate for the grinding and groaning of the truck as it crushed the debris of our past week.

I gave a brief wave and then began to hunt around on the ground for the lids the trash workers always managed to fling amazing distances from the cans.

As my eyes scanned the ground, my neighbor's feet suddenly appeared in my field of vision. "I was wondering if you'd like to come over after work. I'm having a few of the girls in for tea." She spoke in a softer voice now that the noise of the garbage truck had moved on down the street. With a lopsided smile, she disentangled a strand of long brown hair from the hinge of her glasses. Then she bent down to retrieve one of my trash can lids.

"I'm sorry, I don't have time today," I answered automatically. As she handed me the dented lid, I mumbled something about my schedule and the kids. "The girls" were probably all neighbors like her who stayed home with their young children while their husbands worked to pay the bills. I was done with that part of my life and had no wish to be reminded of it. My good mood had finally evaporated.

"Oh, maybe some other day, then?" my neighbor asked hopefully.

"Sure." I turned away, embarrassed that I could not even remember her name. Her black cat was named Zeus; he liked to sleep under the azalea bushes near our front porch. It drove our dog crazy.

"You still need to take Tara for a walk," I reminded Evan as I stepped back into the kitchen and tripped over the dog's leash. The acrid smell of burnt toast hung in the air. A pan crusted with dried egg sat on the stove, and the sink was littered with apple peel and egg residue. I had to clean all of this up before I left for work. I suddenly wondered what made me do it. Instead of handing Alicia a granola bar and letting Evan get his own cereal, I had prepared a Sunday morning feast. But it was Monday, and I didn't have time for this.

As I looked at the basket of laundry I folded when I got up early that morning, I remembered. When I woke up and thought of the new assignment at work, the day seemed to hold a lot of promise. Nothing had happened to change that. The new assignment still held promise. Brian's face flashed in my mind. Lots of promise.

Nothing had changed, except that I had declined a neighbor's invitation. And I didn't even know her, so why should that bother me? I didn't even want to know her. She would be just one more person I'd have to explain things to about Jeff and why we'd moved here. The ones who are married are the worst, because they think they understand, but they don't. Not by a long shot.

By now, I had slipped into an all-out bad mood.

I must have hit every single stoplight on the way to work. When I walked in, I expected Dave to grill me about the Saturday visit right away. But he was nowhere in sight. Well, that would give me time to speak with Mrs. McGregor before I reported to him.

Brittany was typing industriously at her desk. I felt guilty after all the mean things I'd thought about her—here she was, hard at work, while I hadn't even taken off my jacket. Then when I walked closer, I could see that she was instant messaging a friend. At least I hoped it was a friend and not a client, because the message ended with a whole line of smiley faces.

"Where's Dave?" I asked as I hung my coat on a rack of moose antlers by the door. Brittany shrugged, her eyes still glued to the computer screen. "You can call him on the cell."

"Yes. I could have done that from home. The point of having an office is so we have a place to work together so we can occasionally discuss things face-to-face."

She shrugged again. "You can get one of the phones with pictures."

"I'll keep that in mind." I stalked off toward the kitchen to put my lunch in the fridge. On the way back, I realized that I would be doing the same thing to Mrs. McGregor that Dave had forced on me—giving her my presence only by telephone when she really wanted personal contact. Dave would have to pay this woman a visit sometime before this was all over.

I pictured my brother outfitted in the type of puffy shirt and knee-length breeches that Brian had been wearing. While they gave the blacksmith a roguish air, I suspected they would not look so flattering on Dave, who is not tall and has a bit of a paunch. I made a mental note to take plenty of pictures, because they could prove quite useful in future salary negotiations.

The morning wore on. Dave still did not appear, and I found myself filing and working on billing rather than calling Mrs. McGregor. If I was so excited to have this case, so excited that I could hardly sleep, then why was I avoiding the actual work?

I picked up the phone to dial Eileen McGregor. Is *dial* the right term when all the phones in the office have buttons? "Wait," she ordered as she answered, "while I adjust the—"

The phone either hit the counter hard or detonated a large quantity of explosives.

Then her voice returned. "Hello?"

"Mrs. McGregor?" I decided just to just talk really fast so she couldn't interrupt. "DS Investigations has completed the initial survey of the 1776 House, and I am calling to offer an investigative proposal for your approval."

"You're not the man I talked to."

"I am his *secretary*." At this point, I was incredibly grateful that Dave was still AWOL. Brittany, however, seemed quite amused to hear me grovel.

"When is the investigator coming out to the house?" I could picture her frown growing deeper.

"An investigator has already surveyed the site and completed a report which enabled us to create an investigative proposal." Okay, this was not strictly true, but I would write the report soon.

"I didn't see an investigator."

"That's the general idea. Our investigators work undercover to elicit more information."

"Oh." I could hear the wheels turning—anyone who has watched TV usually understands this part and thinks it's pretty cool.

"For an in-depth investigation, we would like to propose that we place one of our agents in the house as a volunteer."

"An excellent idea. We always need more volunteers. In fact, we have a Brownie troop coming next Saturday. Can your investigator help us give house tours?"

"Our investigator will undertake the duties you ask, so long as you pay the required hourly rate."

"But tour guides don't get paid."

"You'll be paying her to investigate, not to give tours."

She paused as if taken aback. "Her? You're sending a woman to investigate this time?"

"We sent a woman last time."

She gave a long sigh. "Oh, very well. But Mr. Sar. . . Sar. . .the nice young man I talked to last week will come out, too. Won't he?"

"Of course." Well, hopefully he would. I tried to think of something to reassure her. "But to ensure the secrecy of the investigation, we will not be able to inform you in advance of his visit. He will come when he thinks the time is right."

"Oh yes. I see."

"So you can expect our investigator on Saturday, coming to volunteer as one of your regular costumed. . . people."

"Docents."

"Er, docents."

"Very good. We have clothing we can supply, so you won't need to worry about that."

"Oh, wonderful." I tried not to sound as dismayed as I felt. This was going to involve witch clothes. I could just tell.

---

Dave finally sauntered in at 3:15 in the afternoon, just when I was leaving. He threw his sports coat at the antlers and missed. "There goes my basketball scholarship." He grinned. "Could you get that for me? And yes, I know you're not my maid. But you're closer."

I reached down, grabbed the coat, brushed the cracker crumbs off the lapel, and hung it neatly on the tip of an antler. "Don't get used to it. I'm just being nice because I have to leave early today."

"You're leaving now?" Dave's grin vanished. "But Evan doesn't get off the bus until four."

"I have to be home by 3:30 to let the termite inspector in."

"But I need to go over three case files. And I can't get the scheduling software to work," Dave whined. "Can't you postpone the inspection?"

I shook my head. "Already have. Twice. We'll lose the warranty if I don't let them in this time."

"Don't you have a neighbor who can let them in?"

"No." I couldn't imagine letting one of them have a key to my house.

"We could send Brittany." He looked around hopefully.

"She leaves for class at noon on Mondays."

He sighed. "You're letting me down, sis."

I set down my bag, walked over to my desk, and pulled a manual from the credenza. "This explains how to use the scheduling software." I tossed it to him.

He caught it cleanly but then looked at it as if he'd forgotten how to read. After a moment, he pried open the cover dubiously. "Karen, please? I'll never figure this out."

He was right. He never would figure it out. "Okay." I plopped back into the computer chair, switched on the computer and monitor, and took off my jacket. "Hold this. And listen, because I'm only going to explain this once."

But I knew better.

## 5

As I got ready to head to the 1776 House, I frowned in the mirror at my short, dark, decidedly modern-looking hair, wishing that, like a doll I had as a kid, I could push a button and pull out locks of long, luxurious, old-fashioned-looking hair. But I couldn't, so I wasn't going to entice Brian with my raven tresses.

And I wasn't even supposed to be thinking about Brian anyway. I was supposed to be thinking up strategies to find the thief.

I arrived at the house about half an hour before it opened to the public. Since everything was locked up, I prepared to knock loudly, just in case Mrs. McGregor didn't have her hearing aid turned up. But just as I raised my hand, the door suddenly swung open inward so that I nearly pummeled the face of the gift shop attendant instead.

"Karen Maxwell?" she asked in an uncertain voice. I think it was the same woman who had greeted us the week before.

"Yes." I shoved my hand into my pocket.

"Eileen told me to expect you this morning. Please come in." She stepped back, her skirts swishing as if they were alive. After she closed the door behind me, she turned and offered her hand. "I'm Ann Bleckenstrauss. I understand you will be volunteering at the house."

"Yes." I looked at her closely, waiting to see if she would say anything more. I had urged Mrs. McGregor not to tell anyone that I was investigating the theft, but I had no way of knowing whether she had taken my advice.

Ann's face split into a kindly, big-toothed smile. "We are always so pleased to have new volunteers. History has a way of being overlooked these days. We have a lovely volunteer tea to thank all our helpers the first Saturday in May, so be sure to put that on your calendar."

"I will." If this woman knew why I was there to work, she was doing a great job of hiding it. "Do you have a special training class that I need to take?" If I had to come back in the evening, Dave would have to pay me double.

"No." Ann sighed. "We are in the process of designing a training manual, but it's not finished yet. So we'll help you learn all you need to know. Now, come along with me and we'll get you a costume." She beckoned toward a set of stairs behind the counter filled with tiny china teacup earrings and elegantly painted fans. The stairs were dark and stacked with boxes, and the landing at the top was even darker and had even more boxes stacked to the ceiling. I held my breath as I squeezed past the boxes to follow Ann into a small room.

She hit the switch on the wall, and a fluorescent light on the ceiling flickered to life, casting a strange bluish glow on boxes, stacked chairs, and miscellaneous household items. A number of hats lay atop the boxes, and the arms of several candelabra stuck out at odd angles, giving the room the appearance of being full of bizarre statues. Or people.

Ann pushed aside a naked mannequin so that

she could open a closet door in the back of the room. "Much too big," she murmured as she pushed hangers around on the rod. "This one might. . ." She pulled out a yellow dress with a cascade of white ruffles. Would Brian find me attractive dressed like a frilly lampshade? I watched with relief as she shook her head and replaced the dress in the closet. Then she pulled out a beautiful blue dress made of some shiny heavy material like silk. She held it up to me. "I think this should work well. Why don't you try it on?"

I didn't have to be urged twice. This dress was so much more attractive than the witch clothes I'd seen on the lady in the kitchen.

I needed Ann's help with the zipper in the back, but it fit beautifully and the rich blue made my skin glow. Though I'd probably have to walk on my toes to keep the hem from dragging, it would be worth it. I looked like a princess. Except for my short hair. I reached up to touch it, suddenly feeling very inadequate.

Ann smiled. "We'll get you a cap to cover your modern hairdo." She rummaged through a box on the closet shelf and produced a small round hat. It reminded me of a shower cap, but at least the ruffles were smaller than those the other women were wearing. And it did cover up the lack of hair.

"Very nice." Ann nodded appraisingly.

I agreed. Only as she started to lead me out of the crowded storeroom did I remember that I was not there to play dress-up but to investigate a theft. Mrs. McGregor told me Ann had keys to the permanent exhibits case, so she had ample opportunity to take the notes. But Mrs. McGregor seemed to think she had no reason to. Could Ann possibly be one of those who wanted the notes removed and had been too shy to voice her opinion in Mrs. McGregor's presence? "Wait up for a minute." I stopped and looked down at the hem of the dress. "This really is too long and I'm afraid I'll step on it. There's not time to shorten it, but I think I could pin it up if you help me."

"Oh, of course. We have a big box of safety pins." Skirts swishing, she squeezed back past me in the tight space and reached for an old cigar box on a shelf.

"I heard," I said in what I hoped was a sufficiently casual tone of voice, "that this house used to have something that belonged to George Washington. But I didn't see it. Is it still here?"

Ann's smile faltered. "Er, it's not on display right now."

"Is it being cleaned? Or did you trade it to another museum?" I tried to make it sound like a joke. "You know, like, 'I'll trade you a Washington for two Jeffersons and a Madison?' "

"Oh." She gave an unconvincing little laugh. "That might have been a good idea." Though she tried to make light of it, I could tell that something was really bothering her. Was she uneasy because the society didn't want people to know the notes were missing? Or was she nervous because she'd taken the notes, perhaps to trade them? Mrs. McGregor had mentioned that Ann wanted the notes placed with the Daughters of the American Patriots for safekeeping. Perhaps she hoped to get something in return, either for herself or for the 1776 House.

"I'd better get back to the gift shop," she murmured,

not looking at me. Without another word, she led the way down the cluttered stairs and back into the gift shop.

The woman with the black hat, the one who had interrupted Mrs. McGregor during my tour, was kneeling in front of a locked glass cabinet, trying various keys in the lock. A look of horror flitted across her features when she saw me.

Had she been caught in the act of another theft?

As she jumped to her feet, the keys jingling malevolently in her hand, she pointed at my outfit. "Ann, you cannot let her wear that gown."

"The other gowns are too big," Ann said with defiance.

"The other gowns don't have *zippers*!" the woman shot right back. "The modern zipper was not invented until 1917! That dress is only suitable for Halloween and high school plays."

Ann frowned, waving away her objection. "No one will notice."

"Yes, they will. They may not say anything to you, but they will notice."

"Then we'll have her stand with her back to the fireplace in the hall during tours. Surely you can't object to that?"

The woman snorted. "I suppose not."

But this would not work at all. If I was trapped in one room all day, I would learn very little. I had expected to be put through some sort of training class, but it appeared that they were so desperate for volunteers that they were just going to dress me up and set me out somewhere.

"I can stand with my back to the fireplace in the kitchen," I offered. The volunteers there might speak more freely than in the house.

"Ha!" the woman sneered. "I'd like to see you try! Patty'd never let you in her kitchen in that polyester monstrosity."

I was starting to feel sorry for the dress.

"The kitchen is not hers," Ann said coldly. Then she turned to me with a kindlier expression. "But Paula is correct in one point, at least. If you wish to work in the kitchen, we'll need to find you a costume more suited to a servant."

Which meant something that didn't fit right and didn't make my eyes sparkle and my skin glow. I could be a peasant woman in a sack dress. I followed Ann back up the stairs with heavy footsteps.

And then I realized what Ann had just said. Not about the clothes—the important part. She referred to the woman we'd just talked to as Paula. I had identified my prime suspect.

And she already seemed to have taken a dislike to me.

When I descended again, clothed in a brown gathered skirt and shapeless green top that made me look as though I'd wrapped a sleeping bag around my middle, Paula Lowell beckoned for me to join her in the corner of the gift shop where she was rummaging through another cabinet.

"I hope you weren't offended by my comments on

the gown," she said, eyeing me frankly as she stood up. Her voice no longer had a hard edge to it, and even her sharp features seemed less hawkish.

I shook my head. I couldn't allow myself to be offended by anything at this point. While I resented the fact that I would look like a colonial whale the next time I saw Brian, I had to get over it if I was going to make any progress.

"That gown was one of the disasters left over from the bicentennial. The house had just opened then, and anything with a long skirt was considered colonial. And from a distance, I suppose the polyester does look like silk, even if it's not period correct. But if you work anywhere near the fire in that getup, it could be a disaster."

"You mean it could catch fire? I hadn't thought about that."

She nodded. "It would melt onto your skin."

That didn't sound at all appealing.

"And," Paula continued gently, "it just isn't correct for the time period—obviously synthetic fabrics did not exist. We want to give visitors a good look into the past, and to do that we need to be as accurate as we can."

"I see." I wasn't quite sure what to say. I wanted her to keep talking, but I didn't want to ask questions—I wanted her to say whatever was on her mind to see if she would give away any clues.

"Do you have any questions?"

So much for that tactic.

"Is there anything else not correct that I should avoid?"

"An excellent question!" She looked from side to side to be sure we were alone before continuing, and when she spoke, her voice was lower. "You'll see a great many inaccuracies here, but we're trying to eliminate them."

Aha! I leaned in closer. "Like what?" I concentrated on the Washington notes, hoping the idea would flow into her mind by osmosis.

"Your cap, for instance."

"My cap?" I felt the gathered circle of fabric on top of my head. This had nothing to do with the missing notes.

"Yes. There is no evidence whatsoever that women ever wore circular caps like that. It's just a simple rendition that later costumers devised. The real caps of the period were shaped in pieces like—"

I needed to get her off the subject of clothing or I would never learn anything of value. I pointed to a display of pencil sharpeners near the cash register. "Is that George Washington crossing the Delaware?"

Her gaze followed my outstretched arm, and a pained expression crossed her features similar to Brian's last week when I'd mentioned Washington. "The gift shop is perhaps the worst of all." She waved toward the jewelry case. "No one walked around with china teacups dangling from their earlobes. And most of the china patterns here are really nineteenth century, in any case."

I pointed to a row of children's books. "That coloring book about Washington looks pretty accurate." It was a lame attempt, admittedly, but I was getting desperate. This woman was obsessed with trivialities. No wonder

Mrs. McGregor resented her intrusion so much.

Paula squinted toward the bookshelves. "Yes, those Dover books are surprisingly good. I know several adults who collect them. Not every detail is reliable, of course, but—"

She had veered off the subject once more. I decided to be blunt. "I heard that you had something of Washington's here in the house, but I didn't see it on my visit last week."

Her eyes narrowed slightly, and though she did not exactly smile, I could almost imagine the laughter of an evil villain inside her head. "We had an artifact *said* to be connected with Washington. It was a ridiculous story, based entirely on conjecture. Fortunately, the artifact has been removed from display."

"What was it? The artifact, I mean."

"A scrap of leather with a few words scribbled on it." She sniffed derisively. "No evidence to connect it with Washington at all."

I tried to remember all that Mrs. McGregor had mentioned in her tour last week. "Well, did George Washington stay here and plan the Battle of the Brandyglass, like the tour guides say?"

"It's the Brandywine. And he most certainly did not plan the battle from the first bedroom," she huffed. "Why, he was in Delaware at the time! How that ridiculous story ever got started, I'll never understand. And it's an absolute travesty to keep repeating it to gullible visitors."

At last I had struck a nerve. Well, I had actually touched off several sore points, but this one finally led in the right direction. "So did Washington ever stay here?"

"No. There's no mention of Barnswallow or the sign of the Bird in Hand—that was the sign Barnswallow used for his business—in any of Washington's copious notes."

"Well, we are on a main trade route," I pointed out, repeating what Brian had said to me last Saturday. "Isn't it possible that—"

"Patty and I spent an entire year combing through every shred of evidence we could find," Paula said firmly. "There was no connection between this site and General Washington." With a dismissive turn of the head, she stalked over to the book section and stuck the George Washington coloring book behind a book of American Girl paper dolls.

And that, apparently, was all that was to be said on the subject. It was just as Mrs. McGregor had told me over the phone—Paula Lowell wouldn't believe anything unless she'd found it herself.

Maybe I could goad Paula into admitting she'd had something to do with the disappearance. "So. . ." I tried to wrest her attention from the coloring books. "I guess it's a good thing that the Washington notes aren't on display anymore."

"Yes."

I waited, hoping she would say more, but she didn't. "I'll bet some people were sad to take out the display, though," I prompted. "The lady who gave us the tour seemed very fond of Washington."

"She'll get over it."

Again I hoped she would say more, but instead she moved the box of pencil sharpeners to the back of a bottom shelf where only an extremely short visitor would be able to see them. She seemed to be avoiding the subject, as if it made her nervous.

I stepped closer to her so that when she stood up, she was looking right in my face. "So, um, did *you* make the decision to remove—"

"I need to see about a laundry demonstration out in the yard," Paula said abruptly. She started toward the door.

"Can I help? It's such a nice day to be working outside, and I don't know enough about the house to give a tour. You wouldn't want me repeating that story about the Battle of the Brandyglass—"

"Brandywine," she corrected automatically.

"Brandywine. See?" I offered a hopeful smile. "I think I'd do much better outside."

"Hurry up, then."

I followed her out the door, wondering what she was trying to hide. The woman who had something to say about every subject had suddenly closed her mouth, and I wanted to know why.

A costumed volunteer with striped socks—Patty, I presumed—was coming out of the kitchen with an enormous black kettle when we stepped into the yard. Paula rushed forward to assist her, and together the two of them hung the kettle from a tripod set off to the side of the kitchen.

"Fetch some water, if you would," Paula ordered, nodding toward a wooden pail sitting next to the kitchen door.

Patty beckoned for me to come closer.

Remembering her harsh demeanor in the kitchen last week, I cringed, expecting to be chastised for something like wearing an inaccurate cap or breathing in a non-period-correct fashion.

"We don't have a well here anymore," Patty whispered with a grin. "So we get water from a tap in the springhouse. Over there." She pointed to the small building of squared-off logs. "At the end of the trough near the far wall."

"Thank you," I whispered back, surprised and pleased to meet this kinder, gentler form of Lowell sister.

It took numerous trips to the springhouse to fill the kettle even half full.

"We had a second pail," Patty explained apologetically, "but it was leaking. John Holbrock took it home to repair it and hasn't brought it back yet."

"And he won't, if you ask me," Paula added with a

sneer. "Probably fixed it and sold it to someone else."

"Is he here today? I can ask him if he brought it back," I offered, anxious to speak with this man of questionable reputation whom Patty had warned Brian about on my last visit. He might certainly have his own motives for taking something valuable connected to George Washington.

"Haven't seen him so far." Paula gave the kettle an appraising look. "One more bucketful should do it."

While I was bringing in water, Paula and Patty piled wood under the kettle and started a fire.

And an argument.

"You were supposed to bring the shifts," Paula said, hands planted on her hips.

"I thought you were going to," Patty answered, "since this demo was your idea."

"You said you—" Paula stopped and turned away from her sister to take the pail of water from me.

"Is there a problem?" I wasn't sure I should interfere, but I did anyway.

"We need clothing to boil for the laundry demonstration. Patty forgot to bring her other shifts."

"What's a shift?" I had a feeling this was something I should know.

Paula grabbed my sleeve and peered up inside as if looking to see whether I had an extra arm hidden somewhere. "Can you believe this? Ann dressed her without a shift."

"A shift is your underwear," Patty half whispered with a little giggle. "It's a white linen garment that looks kind of like a nightgown. You wear it under all your other clothes." She pushed aside a kerchief she had wrapped around her neck, and at the top of her dress, I could see about half an inch of white fabric protruding. Paula held up one of her sleeves to show the white fabric sticking out at the end.

"That's underwear?"

Patty nodded. "And nightwear, too, very often." She looked around and lowered her voice. "They didn't wear underpants or bras in those days."

"Oh."

"Hey, Brian!" Paula called. "Can we borrow your shirt?"

A nervous thrill coursed through me as I whirled around to see Brian coming out of the blacksmith shop.

"Visitors!" Patty hissed with a nod toward the house. A troop of Brownies began to straggle into the yard. "I should get back to the kitchen."

Paula waved for Brian to come closer. "We're setting up a laundry demo, and we have nothing to launder." She laughed. "So give us your shirt."

"Now, Mistress Barnswallow," he said with a grin, "you know I cannot undress in front of guests."

She sighed. "Ah, true sir. T'would taint their impressionable young minds to see a man without his shirt."

He nodded toward me as if just now noticing my presence. His face grew a bit red, and his grin changed to a shy smile. Then he turned abruptly and headed back toward the blacksmith shop before I could find my voice to say hello.

Even though it took a long time for the water to boil, Paula set me to work on the laundry right away, scrubbing at imaginary stains on some old skirts she called petticoats. I rubbed them with pieces of soap that smelled like bacon. I decided to take some home for the next time I had to give the dog a bath. Pork-scented soap might not appeal to me, but canines have different preferences.

It started to get hot out in the sun, and after a while I thought I must have started hallucinating. Before, I'd only been thinking of dogs; now I was seeing one, right there in the yard. It didn't look like our Australian shepherd, Tara, though. This dog was about twice as tall, with short chocolate brown fur and oversized paws. It circled around the laundry setup, running under wet petticoats sagging on a clothesline. Then the dog turned toward the kitchen building, jumped up to the window, snatched something from the ledge, and took off at top speed.

"Ahh!" Patty's squeal probably carried to the next county. "That dog's got my plum cake!"

I was probably closest to the animal, and though I didn't know what a plum cake was, it sounded worth at least an attempt at rescue.

The dog seemed surprised to see me behind him, and I got him cornered against the springhouse. But when I lunged for the cake pan, he flew in the opposite direction.

Brian ran out of the blacksmith shop just as the dog dashed by. He made a grab for the dog's leg, but it slipped through his grasp.

"Let's tempt him with something else," Paula suggested.

"The soap?" I remembered that commercial where

a dog goes crazy over the scent of bacon.

Paula shook her head. "Patty," she called toward the kitchen, "get a piece of salt pork."

"What?" Patty yelled back indignantly. "Are we feeding this animal dinner now?"

Returning to the chase, I saw that the dog had stopped in the center of the yard as if uncertain where to go next. I snuck up behind him slowly and was pleased to see that Brian was coming at him from the opposite side. As if by unspoken agreement, we lunged at the same moment toward the four-legged thief.

The animal jumped from between us, disappearing in a blur of brown fur. Brian and I collided, my head hitting his shoulder, and we collapsed in the grass. I suppose it should have been an awkward moment, but all I could do was laugh.

Brian grinned as he jumped to his feet and reached out a hand to help me up. "Brian Kieffer. Pleased to meet you!"

I brushed my hand across my apron to make sure I wouldn't offer him a sweaty palm. "I'm Karen Maxwell. I'm new."

"But you look familiar. . . . Have you been here—"

Patty's voice interrupted our introduction. "He's headed for the house!"

Brian and I both ran toward the main house but had no hope of catching up with the canine in overdrive. He disappeared through the open door into the gift shop.

"I don't think Mrs. McGregor is going to like this," I murmured.

"You're right," Brian answered, his face growing suddenly sober.

As if to confirm our prediction, panicked screams immediately erupted from the house.

"Eeahhh!"

"What is that—get it—get it out!"

"Keep it off the rug—its paws might be muddy."

"Keep it off the floor—its nails might scratch the wood!"

"What?" I muttered in disbelief. "Do they expect the poor dog to levitate?"

The sober expression on Brian's face immediately changed back to a grin. "Yes. I think they do."

I tried not to laugh—the ladies inside really seemed to be experiencing a great deal of distress—but it was all so ridiculous. My muffled laugh came out as an extremely unappealing snort, which was actually even funnier.

Two young boys ran across the yard and demanded to know what the commotion was all about.

Laughing, Brian pointed toward the open door. "There's a wild dog inside that's stolen the cook's plum cake. See if you can catch him!"

"I don't think that's going to improve the situation any," I pointed out. "Their shoes were muddier than the dog's paws."

"Were they? I didn't notice." Brian looked remorseful. But only for a moment. He sputtered into a laugh again as Paula stalked toward us with Patty in her wake.

"What's so funny?" Paula demanded. "If you had smelled that plum cake, you wouldn't be in such a good mood."

"I'm sorry, Patty." Brian tried to bring his mirth

under control. "I'm sure you worked hard on that cake. That's the third stray dog we've had through here this year, at least."

I blinked. "The third?"

Patty nodded. "Or fourth. I actually don't mind. It lends an air of authenticity to the site. Since county regulations won't permit us to have farm animals here, we should have some wildlife around."

"True." Brian nodded. "This sort of animal roguery is quite period correct. They don't usually get into the house these days, but I'll bet it happened all the time back in Josiah's day."

"Stray dogs running through the house?" I asked incredulously.

"Dogs, chickens, pigs—sure. They had to keep the doors open for light and air. I'm sure there were animals all over the place. Well, ladies." He glanced toward the sun as it sank lower in the western sky. "It's getting on towards time to leave. I'd better start closing up." He nodded a farewell and started back toward the blacksmith shop with long strides.

I watched him, long hair streaming behind him and dirty shirt billowing in the breeze, striding confidently toward the fire and anvil as if he spent his life in front of them. Brian Kieffer seemed to belong back in the eighteenth century. It was impossible to imagine him doing something as mundane as driving a car or talking on a phone.

Patty lightly sprinkled the fire under the kettle with water and began to separate the burning embers.

"Should I start cleaning up this display?" I asked her.

Patty cast an appraising gaze at the laundry kettle. "Let's let this cool a bit before we empty it out. You can help me with the dishes."

I sighed as I followed Patty back to the kitchen and wondered if next Saturday Brian might need an assistant in the blacksmith shop.

~

I washed a box full of dirty bowls, cutting boards, knives, and spoons in a basin in the springhouse and watched for Brian as I carried the box back to the kitchen. But the door to the blacksmith shop was closed and no smoke came from the chimney. Inside the kitchen, I found Paula helping Patty scrub the worktable with a rag. "Should we ask Brian to help get that kettle down?" I asked hopefully as I set down the box of clean but wet dishes.

"He's already left," Patty announced as she reached out to take a knife from the box. "You didn't dry these?" She held up the knife accusingly. "They'll rust away to nothing!"

I cringed.

"He had a meeting at church, I think," Paula said as she tossed me a dish towel. "Steel rusts quickly. Remember, in a pinch you can dry things on your apron."

Patty sighed. "It seems like Brian's always got a meeting of some sort or another."

"What kind of meetings?" I tried to make the question casual as I inspected a knife for signs of rust.

Paula and Patty exchanged significant glances. I guess I didn't succeed in the attempting-to-appear-only-casually-interested department.

"He leads the church youth groups—plans the kids' outings, coaches basketball, runs a drama club," Paula explained.

"It doesn't much matter, just too many meetings," Patty added.

I nodded in agreement. Church was so dull. I figured I would go crazy if I had that many "church things" to do.

"He needs to get out," Patty continued. "Spend time with adults."

"He volunteers here," I pointed out.

"Yes," Patty said in agreement, "but he spends most of his time here teaching kids, too. He's always teaching, always working. I don't think he ever does anything just for fun."

I wiped a spoon dry with the towel Paula had given me. "He seems to enjoy being here."

"I suppose," Patty mused as she added some bowls to a stack on the shelf. "But we never see him smile much anymore."

Paula pointed toward the blacksmith shop with the handle of a broom. "He never laughs like he used to."

"He laughed today," I said. "When we were chasing the dog."

Paula stopped sweeping and leaned on the broom handle for a moment. "You know, he did."

"That's right." Patty grinned at me. "You must be a good influence on him."

"I didn't make him laugh. It was the dog." I smiled, but I really wished it *had* been me.

"I think you should ask him out," Paula said matter-of-factly as she swept the dust over the threshold. "I would myself if I weren't so old."

"Karen might be married, you know," Patty pointed out.

"Not anymore," I said, almost to myself. It sometimes still seemed hard to believe that the life Jeff and I had shared was gone forever.

"So you should ask him out, then," Paula concluded.

"I assume that means he's not married." Butterflies started to career wildly around my insides.

"His wife died five years ago," Patty said softly. "She was a lovely woman."

Paula rested the broom in the corner and dusted her hands on her apron. "That's her picture on the front of our brochure. Have you seen it?"

The butterflies in my stomach fell with a crashing thud. I had indeed seen the brochure, which featured a picture of a smiling and very beautiful young woman sitting at a spinning wheel. I wasn't beautiful, and I didn't even really know what a spinning wheel did, much less how to use one. No way was I in this woman's league.

"Patty, if you're not married, maybe you should ask him out," I suggested. I was willing to bet that Patty could spin.

Patty offered a gentle smile. "I did, once. I asked him if he would go with me to a symposium at Belair Mansion. I don't like to drive at night."

I attempted to picture Brian driving a car and still could not. Then I tried to imagine Paula or Patty getting behind the wheel in their starched caps and layers of clothing and couldn't manage that, either.

"Well, think about it, anyway," Paula urged. "You must admit he's good-looking!"

"No argument there," I answered quickly.

Too quickly, apparently, because Paula let out an immediate huff of laughter. "Well, how did you find your first day?"

"Tiring," I answered truthfully as I rubbed my back.

"If you wear stays under your shortgown, they'll help support your back."

"Good idea." I nodded, even though I had no idea what she was talking about. Since both sisters seemed to have accepted me, I decided this would be a good time to question them about the missing notes again. "I understand there are some inaccurate stories circulating about the 1776 House, and I don't want to repeat them. The stories about Washington, for example." Remembering how Paula suddenly clammed up on the subject back in the gift shop, I decided to try a different angle. "There is a uniform in the bedroom upstairs. Is it one of his?"

"Heavens, no." Paula chuckled as she seated herself on a bench by the window. "If we had a uniform of Washington's, it would be under lock and key."

"With alarms and bulletproof glass," Patty added as she picked at a drop of wax that had hardened on the table.

"Maybe that's what they needed for the Washington notes," I suggested, watching Paula closely for a reaction. "Mrs. McGregor told me they were stolen."

Paula's grin vanished. "That's ridiculous," she said in a harsh voice. "No one would want to steal that worthless scrap of leather."

"She thinks they were stolen?" Patty said thoughtfully. "I suppose that is possible. Remember, Ann was always warning us that we should send them to a museum with better security."

Paula snorted in derision. "Ann Bleckenstrauss just thought that if we gave the notes to the DAP, they'd be so grateful that they'd make her a member of their board and invite her to their big national meetings."

"So you weren't told they were stolen?"

Patty shook her head. "No one has actually told us what happened to them. They were simply not on view one Saturday. The case was empty. And then they removed the case. I assumed it was a decision of the museum committee. Ann is the chair. You should ask her."

"I hate to upset her if she believes the notes were stolen." Again I watched for Paula's reaction.

Her scowl deepened. "She has no reason to be upset. The notes were worthless. Now we can get rid of all the Washington nonsense and stop lying to the public."

"Lying?" I prompted, trying not to betray the excitement I felt. Paula would get worked up and let something slip—I just knew it.

"George Washington did *not* rip off the bottom of a chair to scribble on a scrap of leather." Paula drummed on the table to accent her words. "He was far too much of a gentleman to go around ripping up furniture."

"He might have had a slave do it," Patty mused in a quiet voice as she stared at the lone candle burning in the center of the scarred worktable. "Or maybe a subordinate brought him the leather without telling him where he got it."

Paula paused, clearly taken by surprise. Then she shook her head. "We've already established that Washington never came near this house. It's all an insidious lie to trick the public. Instead, we should focus on the real reasons to visit the site."

"Such as?" I prompted again.

Paula smiled at her sister. "Such as award-winning living history interpretations."

My first inclination was to ask who on earth would give awards for such things, but I kept my mouth shut.

"Patty won the Brent Award for Excellence in Historical Interpretation and Education," Paula announced with obvious pride.

"And the site has much more," Patty added quickly, her face coloring. "A great many period-correct demonstrations. Brian's smithy and John's carpentry, and the laundry we did today, for example."

Paula nodded. "People can come and learn the real history now. The history of real people. Not some lies about Washington."

"So you're glad the notes are gone?" I asked.

Paula nodded. "Yes, absolutely."

"I think," said Patty slowly, "that it's for the best."

That was probably enough for now. If I kept pestering them with questions about the notes, they might realize I had more than a casual interest in them.

"Oh, I didn't realize what time it was." I cast a belated look at my watch. "I'll see you next week," I said as I started to head out into the yard.

Patty raised her hand to stop me. "I have an old pair of stays that might fit you," she said. "I'll bring them for you to try on."

"Great!" If I was pretending to be interested in this stuff, I would have to pretend to be excited by these sorts of details. And eventually I might even find out what she was talking about.

## 7

Taking the lead on a case might be interesting, but it put me way behind in my other work. On Tuesday afternoon I was still finishing up the Monday paperwork. After reading one of the reports, I sighed in frustration and took it out to Brittany. "You need to fix the spelling mistakes in this." I held out the sheaf of paper.

"But Dave wanted me to finish this proposal," she whined, pointing at her computer screen.

"He also promised to have this report to the client yesterday. And in case you haven't noticed, it's today." I dangled the pages in front of her face.

"It's always today," she grumbled.

"And our reports are always late. Now fix this so we can send it out this afternoon."

She reached out to grasp the pages between her thumb and forefinger gingerly, as if fearful that some of the spelling errors might leap off onto her lap and leave ink stains on her miniskirt. "I don't know what the problem is. I ran spell-check three times."

"If you look up the file, I think you'll see that spell-check *is* the problem. Our client is Mr. Moran, not Mr. Moron. He is not concerned about the business of clowning but rather with something he calls corporate cloning. And unless I'm greatly mistaken, he lives on Dunhill Street, not Dunghill Street."

"I didn't realize."

"Check it against the file. Every time, please. Our

agency's reputation rests on your proofreading skills." That wasn't actually true, since I proofread everything before it goes out. If Dave ever sent out one of her reports before I read it over, our agency's reputation would rest somewhere down near the earth's inner core.

"Okay." She looked around the desk expectantly. "So where is the file?"

"Let's see. . ." I squinted as my eyes scanned cabinets placed strategically throughout the office so that they rested on support beams that hadn't been damaged by termites. "Client file cabinets, watercooler, client file cabinets, coffeemaker, client file cabinets. . . I think the file is probably in the refrigerator."

It could have been, actually. I did once leave a file in the refrigerator after I got distracted by an exploding bowl of chili in the microwave. Fortunately, that was before we hired Brittany, so it was not part of her corporate memory.

With an exaggerated sigh that revealed her days of adolescence were not so far in the past, Brittany heaved herself to her feet and trundled over to the nearest file cabinet, wobbling a bit as her platform sandals slipped on the worn floorboards.

Confident that a college preparatory education had at least given her the ability to find alphabetized files, I went back to my own desk. I only had a few minutes left to finish up a schedule before I needed to head out to drop some signed statements in the overnight drop box.

In order to get there before the pickup, I would have to leave in three minutes. At least Dave wasn't here to delay me.

"Have you seen the charger for my cell phone?"

Dave asked as he flung open the office door.

"No." Of course, I hadn't looked for it, either. It could easily be hidden among the stacks of paper and debris in his office.

He pulled the phone from his pocket, shook it a few times, looked at it in disgust, and then set it on my desk. "I tried to call to tell you that I need you to fill me in on the McGregor case before you leave."

He made it sound as if I were leaving to have my nails done rather than leaving to deliver his paperwork.

I glanced at the clock. "I have two minutes."

"Talk fast," he ordered.

"Can't we go over this tomorrow?"

"Mrs. McGregor has called me six times today." He held up the cell phone. "And she wants to know if she should send more money. I need something to tell her."

"Perhaps you should tell her to talk to me."

He shook his head. "No, she'll feel better if she hears a report from me."

As much as I hated to admit it, I realized he was right. "Okay, in a nutshell: I think she's right—I think Paula Lowell most likely took the notes. But there may be others at the site who wanted to see them disappear, too, like her sister. And there's another suspect I need to learn about, a guy who has stolen things in the past to resell." I paused to mentally go over my conversations from Saturday. "Ann Bleckenstrauss, whom Mrs. McGregor doesn't suspect at all, could possibly have removed the notes to give to another historical organization, some big outfit in DC." I paused again, bothered by the sensation that I was missing something. Something obvious. But

I couldn't think what it was. I shrugged. "That's what I've got for now. So why don't you tell her you've got four suspects under consideration." I glanced at my watch. "And we're now down to one minute."

Dave crossed his arms in front of his chest. "Okay, so why are you so sure it's this Low woman?"

"Lowell. And I think she took the notes because she very obviously wanted them gone. And she has access to lots of keys and cabinets, and all parts of the house and grounds."

"And no one else does?"

"Well, Ann does. Which is why I think we have to consider her a suspect. But something tells me she would never go against Mrs. McGregor's wishes."

"Never discount a suspect. Some of the best actors in the world never set foot on a stage." He didn't wag his finger at me as he spoke, but I had the distinct impression of the gesture nevertheless.

As much as I doubted that he was right in this case, I would try to follow the lesson anyway. "I guess you're right. I'll keep a close watch on Ann, too." I reached for my purse in the bottom desk drawer. "Now I'd better go, or I'll miss the pickup."

"Will you be back in today?"

"No. I have to get home to the kids." He should know that by now.

He fiddled with the clip on his cell phone. "It might be better if you talk to her. After I do."

"Talk to who?"

He waved the cell phone. "You know. The 'hysterical society' lady."

"Mrs. McGregor?" I grinned. "I think you're afraid of her."

"Annoyed and afraid are two different things. Just call her soon, okay?"

My enjoyment of Dave's unusual discomfiture gradually receded as I jogged down the block and turned the corner onto Main Street, headed to the large stone building with enough offices and shops to justify the presence of an overnight delivery drop box. Our office was just outside the cute, trendy, refurbished strand of old stone buildings that made up the former mill town. It's nearly always impossible to find a parking place (and I hate to parallel park in a minivan anyway), so unless the weather is unbearable, I always just run down to the box—or walk if I leave with enough time.

Today I almost didn't make it. The bells of St. Patrick's were chiming the quarter hour as I rounded the corner, their ponderous, mournful tolls reminding me just how late I was. The uniformed pick-up guy was already unlocking the box when I ran up.

"Just in time," he said with a smile as he reached for the stack of envelopes I had tucked under my arm.

"Thanks." I smiled back, grateful. And yet I was suddenly bothered, too. I turned to walk back to where my van was parked near the office.

Why should I be bothered by the friendly smile of an overnight delivery guy? It hit me as I watched a couple holding hands in front of a shop featuring an unlikely array of original art prints, stained-glass works, and collectible Star Wars figurines. In my report to Dave, I had not mentioned Brian as a suspect. I had not even considered the possibility.

Yes, he was attractive, considerate, funny, and, like the delivery guy, had a nice smile. But he was also a suspect. He clearly wanted the Washington notes taken away. He was at the site every Saturday and had the trust of the others. He probably had keys just like Paula and Ann. Maybe not, but probably. That would be one thing easy to ascertain, at least.

He had as much motive as Paula. I needed to determine if he had the opportunity. And while I felt fairly certain he was not the type to stoop to dishonest means to achieve a goal, Brian might well be a good actor, just as Dave had warned. Hadn't Paula mentioned something about a drama club?

A cold wind hit me as I turned the corner to head back.

---

"Pepperoni and hamburger?" Evan's eyes widened to the size of paper plates as he lifted the lid on the pizza box. "You ordered both?" He reached for a slice with eager hands.

"Would you like a root beer?" I held up a cold can, hoping that the sight of his favorite food and drink would distract him from the ongoing squabbles with his sister that increasingly ate into our time together.

"In the can! Excellent." He set down his pizza and scurried over to wrench a can free from the plastic rings.

Alicia uttered an exaggerated sigh. "Use a plate, you plebeian. You're getting grease all over the table."

"She's calling me names again," Evan accused, pointing his root beer at her. "You shouldn't call me a pleb-whatever-it-was."

Alicia smiled smugly as she dabbed the excess oil from her pizza with a paper towel. "You don't even know what the word means."

"I don't have to. If you used it, it was bad."

"Shows what you know." Her smug grin broadened. "I did not use a bad—"

I held up my hand to signal both of them to stop. "That's enough, you two." I frowned at a smear of tomato sauce on the sleeve of my new white sweater.

Though I wanted to keep my tone light, I failed miserably. My voice came out sounding harsh and mean. I had tried to start off our Friday evening on a positive note, even renting two movies that bored me to pieces but that I knew the kids loved. Blown, all of it. Their bickering brought out the domineering mom in me, and once again all chance of friendship and camaraderie was out the window. They always seemed to have so much fun on the weekends when they were with their dad. But I couldn't seem to maintain "fun" for more than thirty seconds.

And things were only going to get worse when I told them what I had planned for Saturday.

A chair scraped back across the floor as Evan sat down with his pizza. "What's a plebeian?"

"Look it up," I answered automatically as I dabbed a wet paper towel on the sleeve of my sweater.

"Not with those hands," Alicia admonished. "You'll get grease all over the dictionary."

"So?" Evan countered. "It's *my* dictionary. Aunt Helen gave it to *me* for kindergarten graduation."

"But we all use it," Alicia wailed as she followed him over to the bookshelves in the family room. "And anyway, it's not fair because she didn't give me anything when I graduated."

Evan plucked the book from the shelf. "Guess she likes me better than you."

I threw down the paper towel and stepped over to him. "And if she could hear you right now, she wouldn't like either one of you. Listen to yourselves." I took the book from his hands and held it up so they could both get a good look at it. "You're fighting over a paperback dictionary that cost three dollars and ninety-five cents."

Evan's mouth gaped open. "Aunt Helen only spent four dollars on my graduation gift?"

I glared at him. "The point is that she cared enough about you to take the time to get you a gift at all. And she took time to think of a good gift. A gift you could use."

"A dictionary is a pretty lame gift for a five-year-old."

"I'd say it was a pretty good gift if it's something we are still using all these years later." I sighed. I knew they still didn't get it, but I didn't know how to explain what was wrong about this whole argument. "You need to be nicer to each other," I added lamely. "Family members are supposed to stick together." There had to be a better reason than that. I tried to think back to something my mom or a Sunday school teacher might have said. "Love thy enemy," was the only thing that came to mind. I decided that while the "love" directive was admirable, Evan did not need to be encouraged to think of his sister as the enemy.

I probably should have sent them to Sunday school so a teacher could explain why they should be nice to each other. I'm afraid they just might be too set in their ways to learn that lesson now.

Alicia reached for the book in my hand. "We used to have another dictionary. A big one, with a hard cover."

"And pictures," Evan added. "Yeah, where is it?"

A sick feeling grew in the pit of my stomach. "It was your dad's," I said softly. "Probably from when he was in college."

"So it's at the other house now?"

I swallowed over a lump in my throat. "I guess so." Evan probably wished he was with his dad and his new wife right now. At the house back in the old neighborhood with Charlie and Grant to play with, where they had about ten times as many video games and a pool table.

"A plebeian is 'one of the common people,' or 'a vulgar, coarse person,'" Alicia read from the dictionary.

"Did you really mean to call your brother 'vulgar'?" I asked her.

She looked at me for a moment as if to say that indeed she did. But then she shook her head. "No."

"Evan, are you okay with being considered one of the common people?" I asked as I turned to him.

He shrugged. "I guess. It just means I'm normal."

"Exactly." I smiled. Maybe the night wouldn't be so bad after all.

"I'm normal," Evan continued thoughtfully. "I think sports are good and plays are stupid."

I sighed. "Your pizza is getting cold." I started back to the table and had just opened my mouth to take a bite when the dryer buzzed. It was a loud, obnoxious, insistent drone that usually made me wish I used a clothesline.

"Did you remember to wash my uniform?" Evan asked with a sudden look of concern. I don't think he actually cared whether it was clean, but he remembered the time I forgot to dry it and he had to run up and down the field with wet shorts clinging to his legs.

"I haven't yet. But you don't have a game until Monday."

"I don't have a Saturday game?" His face was incredulous.

"Not this week." I took a deep breath and paused on my way to the dryer. I might as well get this over with. "So before Alicia's drama rehearsal tomorrow, we're going back to the 1776 House."

"What?"

Though I had almost reached the laundry closet and could no longer see Evan, I could imagine him spewing a spray of food bits across the table with his outburst.

"Eeww!" Alicia confirmed my suspicion. At least I hoped her noise of disgust was directed at her brother's mouth rather than the prospect of spending the day at the 1776 House.

I took my time folding the clothes to give them a few minutes to get used to the idea.

"Why are we going back to that house?" Alicia asked as she wiped her hands on a napkin.

"There are a number of different reasons," I said quickly, busying myself with throwing out stray bits of trash and wiping up counters. I had rehearsed my answers but still wasn't very comfortable with them. The two main reasons—working for Dave and wanting to see Brian—were not matters I felt I should reveal, at least not yet. "Evan has to do a project on Maryland history, so I thought he should visit the site again, and that would give him ideas for his project."

"The project isn't due until December," Evan objected in a morose tone.

"I think it will be more fun to go now, while the weather is so nice. And they promised a demonstration of carpentry, which I'd like to see." Mainly because the carpenter was John Holbrock, one of the suspects I had yet to meet. But of course I couldn't tell Evan that.

"I don't want to see it."

"Well, the site needs volunteers, and I think we should help out once in a while."

"We helped out last time. We bought sodas from the gift shop."

"Evan, you need to think about someone other than yourself for a change." I felt like a hypocrite saying that, since it was my job that was making him go, but a little volunteer work wouldn't hurt him.

Alicia stood abruptly. "I think it will be good for us. We'll get in touch with our ancestors." She threw her paper plate in the trash. "Do you have any long skirts from when you were a girl?"

"Girls weren't wearing long skirts when I was a girl. How old do you think I am?"

"We'll both need long skirts." She looked at Evan and giggled. "And he'll need short pants. I'm going online to see what we should be wearing. What did that lady say the date of the house was again?"

"Seventeen seventy-six would be my guess."

"Oh yeah." Alicia giggled again as she scuttled up the stairs to use the computer in my room.

Evan rolled up his paper plate. Then he looked at me with defiance glittering in his blue eyes. "I'm not going."

I came over to the table, sat down next to him, leaned close, and spoke in a low voice. "I think volunteer service hours can earn you video games."

"Really?" His eyes momentarily lit with joy, but the glow was soon replaced by a look of suspicion. "New ones?" He knew that whenever I bought him games, they came from yard sales or, at best, the used section of the store.

But I was willing to go the extra mile this time. "Major League Baseball, Rabid Raccoon Racing. . ." I listed titles that I had seen him eyeing in the electronics department.

The look of joy returned. For a brief moment, it was like Christmas morning the year before Jeff announced that he was leaving. The Christmas where we seemed to have everything, and Evan was just old enough to understand and be overwhelmed by it all.

He nodded. "Okay. But none of those weird baggy short pants."

"You can wear your regular clothes," I agreed. "But I should tell you this won't be the only visit. You'll probably need to go back another time or two. Your participation will be rewarded, however."

"What is Alicia going to get?"

"Alicia is going to get what she always wants—a chance to act in front of an audience. I'll probably buy her some costume stuff."

Evan looked at me for a moment. "Are you doing this because you really like history?"

I fought the urge to look away. I really did not want

to lie to him. "It's complicated," I finally answered.

He unrolled his plate and reached for another slice of pizza. "That's what I thought you'd say."

"I will explain someday, though." I kissed the top of his head. "I promise."

## 8

"Mom, you're not going to let him bring that soccer ball into the 1776 House, are you?" Alicia stood outside the car, hands on her hips, looking every inch the bossy older sister.

"Soccer is an old game, invented by the ancient Chinese." Evan looked down his nose at Alicia. "I looked it up. So they had soccer in colonial days." He dribbled the ball around his sister, taking care to keep just out of the reach of her legs.

"I don't think Mrs. McGregor would appreciate being hit in the head with a goal kick. And she probably wouldn't like it if you hit any of the visitors, either. Even the first graders." I pointed to indicate that he needed to return the ball to the van.

"Who's Mrs. McGregor?" Alicia asked.

Oops. I didn't want the kids treating her differently than any of the other adults on the site. "One of the ladies in charge," I said quickly.

"The one that dresses like a witch?" Evan flicked the ball up into his arms with a little kick that I always found rather amazing.

"No, that's Patty. And she doesn't act like a witch, at least not most of the time. But if she asks you to wash any dishes, make sure you dry them thoroughly. Put the ball back."

"But what about times when there aren't any visitors?" he persisted.

"Tell you what, *I'll* put the ball in the van." Before

he could protest, I snatched the ball and locked it away. When I turned back around, Alicia was gone.

"Alicia?" I called somewhat forlornly as I waded through the gravel toward the house. How was I going to keep track of the developments in this investigation if I couldn't even keep track of my own children for more than a minute at a time? I had already struggled into my 1776 costume, but I still had to get the kids dressed before the house opened to the public.

"She must have gone around to the back," Evan announced.

"How do you know?" While mothers were supposed to be able to see out of the backs of their heads, I didn't think brothers were supposed to be able to see through buildings.

"There." Evan pointed to the grass at the side of the house.

As we walked closer, I could see a scarf on the ground. At least, I thought it was a scarf. When I picked it up, I could see it was a pillowcase, part of the eight-hundred-thread-count Egyptian cotton sheet set my mother had given me for Christmas. The pillowcase had been cut open and trimmed to a triangular shape.

"Alicia!" I stalked around the corner of the house in search of my vandal.

But instead of finding Alicia in a nearly empty yard, I found a scene of activity almost resembling a carnival. At the center was a long table covered with a blue cloth and heaped with cakes, pies, and cookies of assorted colors. Another table, with a red cloth, held artfully arranged baskets of books, gourmet foods, toiletries, and other prizes, all wrapped in very noncolonial-looking cellophane and crowned with big bows. An array of carpenters' tools surrounded a bench off to one side. There was no sign of the previous week's laundry demonstration, thankfully, but a small fire had been built, and near that stood a collection of metal tubes and sticks with string tied to them.

Patty came out of the kitchen, tying the ribbons of a straw hat under her chin. Paula followed, adjusting the brim of her big ugly black hat.

"You missed one." Patty pointed to a cherry tree at the corner of the house, where a red balloon fluttered on a short string.

Paula pulled a long, wicked-looking pin from her hat, marched over to the tree, and stabbed the life out of the balloon with a gentle *pop*. "Balloons." She sniffed in disgust as she carried the shattered remnants back in her fingers. "Can you believe it? They didn't exist until 1847. Goodyear didn't even develop a practical process to vulcanize rubber until 1843."

"Good morning, Karen." Patty smiled at me. "I have those stays for you."

Stays, I had learned, were like a corset. My enthusiasm for wearing them was a great deal less than she seemed to think it should be.

"I brought my daughter, Alicia, and my son, Evan," I said quickly, hoping she would forget about forcing me to wear disfiguring undergarments. At the mention of her name, Alicia scurried over with a look of eager anticipation that I rarely saw on her face anymore. I decided to wait until later to chastise her about the ruined pillowcase.

"How d'ye do, Alicia?" Patty reached out a hand in greeting.

Alicia shook it a little uncertainly.

"I think she would like to help you in the kitchen, if that's okay," I suggested.

"Of course." Patty threw her arm around Alicia's shoulders as if they'd been best buddies for years. "We'll see if we can round up some suitable clothing for you before the public arrives."

Alicia pulled off her backpack, which I could now see was stuffed to overflowing with fabric. "I put together an outfit," she said shyly, "but it's probably not very good." She began to pull things out and lay them on the grass in front of her. "I didn't have a shift, but I thought this nightgown would work, since it won't show much."

"Good thinking. That will surely do for today."

"And I cut the bottom off a dress to make a petticoat."

I winced. The dress was a hand-me-down from her older cousin, but it was a very expensive hand-me-down, and I'd hoped she could wear it for eighth-grade graduation next year. Oh well. . .

"And I trimmed off parts of this robe to make a bedgown."

Patty nodded appreciatively. "You've really done your research, young lady."

I squinted at the robe, which did not look at all familiar.

"And I made an apron out of a sheet," Alicia concluded with pride.

"What?" My attention shifted abruptly from the cut-up bathrobe to the remains of sheet that Alicia held up in her hands.

"It was big enough that I could cut the ties and everything out of one piece." She smiled sheepishly at Patty. "'Cause I don't know how to sew."

Patty fingered the material in her hands. "You'll want to finish off those rough edges, though, so they don't fray. I can show you how to do that much."

As the two new buddies picked up the clothing and started toward the house, I finally found my voice. "You cut up my sheets? My good sheets? Why didn't you cut up your own sheets?"

"Mine have unicorns on them." Alicia glanced at the fabric in my hands. "Oh, you found my neckerchief."

Patty smothered a laugh, in deference to the look of anguish on my face. "Let's get you changed. The house will open to the public soon, and the bake sale always draws an early crowd." Patty turned to me. "Do you want to come in and try on those stays now?"

"I need to get Evan settled first." I hurried away from her before she could find some reason that it was absolutely essential for me to wear a device that would squeeze all the air out of my lungs and rearrange my internal organs.

Evan hadn't even wanted to come, let alone volunteer, so it would be difficult to get him dressed in colonial clothes. I had brought along a pair of his pants that were too short, cut off at the knees, and hoped I could talk him into wearing those at least, and he could just go shirtless and barefoot.

But he was nowhere in sight. While there were many places he might have run off to hide, the first place I searched was the blacksmith shop. I told myself it was because he had a good time on our last visit and not because I was eager to see Brian.

My insides got all fluttery as I drew close to the brick building. If he gave me that smile again, the sharing-the-moment-of-the-dog-running-wild-with-a-stolen-cake-make-my-heart-turn-flips smile, I just might take Paula's advice and ask him out. I might.

I didn't know if I could really do it. I hadn't been on a date—with anyone other than Jeff—since high school. And I had never asked a boy out.

Boy? A boy? I was thirty-four years old, had two kids, and had been married for almost ten years. I was not looking for a boy this time. If I was going to date again, I needed to find a man.

I stopped on the stone threshold of the blacksmith shop. Evan and Brian were talking in low voices near the forge, Evan looking down shyly from time to time, but still engaged, not trying to back away.

I decided I needed a man at least six feet tall, with dark wavy hair, clear blue eyes, and the muscular physique of someone who threw heavy iron implements around on a regular basis.

My insides now felt so fluttery that I wished I had agreed to wear the corset/stays device around my middle just to hold my stomach still. Brian was just the man to ask out, to spend time with, and to laugh with. To share that awful-yet-exciting first date experience with.

But there was no reason on earth why he would want to go out with me.

I decided Evan was doing just fine on his own. I slowly stepped away from the doorway back into the yard.

"Karen, is that you?" The rich, rumbling low voice did not come from my nine-year-old son. I stepped inside the shop.

The smell of smoke, oil, and a familiar but un-named metallic substance hung heavily in the air.

Brian waited until I was practically right in front of him before he spoke again. "I told your son we could really use his help with all the extra activities we've got going today, and he's agreed to be my assistant."

Evan bounced up and down a little with his newfound sense of importance. "But Brian said the other kids will listen to what I say better if I'm dressed like him. Y'know, if I have to tell them to stay back from the fire or not to touch the sharp tools."

"Sharp tools?" I looked at the dull hammers and blunt tongs.

Brian nodded toward the doorway. "I'm going to spend part of the afternoon on a woodworking demonstration with John out in the yard." He grinned at Evan. "And there are always visitors who want to touch the sharp blades."

Evan pointed at Brian but looked at me. "So can you make me some clothes like his? I know you can sew."

"Yes, but, um, do you mean now?" I looked at Brian's shirt, leather apron, and breeches. "I might be able to make the apron from some fake leather left over from your Native American festival costume, but. . ."

Brian winced but quickly covered it with a smile. "He doesn't need an apron. Just short pants and a shirt should do for now.

I looked around the shop, at the massive wood

beams, aged brick floor, giant leather bellows, and array of black iron tools. "I guess fake leather isn't the look you're trying for here, is it?"

His smile widened. "I'm glad you understand. So many people don't. It's better to do without than to make do with something blatantly inaccurate. And fake leather is usually pretty—"

"Fake-looking. I know." I turned to Evan. "I've got a pair of short pants for you, and as Brian says, you can do without the rest for today."

"We've probably got an extra shirt in the attic somewhere, and maybe even a pair of shoes. I'll have John take a look."

I turned back to Brian so fast it made me dizzy. That John would most likely be John Holbrock, my third suspect. "I can ask John myself," I offered quickly, "if you tell me what he looks like."

"Well, sure." Brian stopped. "He's about my height, hair's not so long, though, kind of medium brown color. He usually wears glasses and a cocked hat. What we now call a tricorn."

"Okay." I turned to run out the door. But though I searched the kitchen, house, and everywhere in between, neither Paula, Patty, Ann, nor Mrs. McGregor had seen John. And now it was nine o'clock and the site would be opening. No one had time to look for a shirt. I walked out to the van to pick up the pants I had shortened for Evan.

Just as I shut the van door, I saw a pickup truck pull into a spot in the back corner. The driver seemed to take an unusually long time getting out. He was wearing colonial clothing, stood about average height, and had brown hair showing under his tricorn hat, just as Brian had described.

And I had the perfect excuse to introduce myself. "Hello!" I hurried over to greet him with the enthusiasm that Paula, Patty, Brian, and Ann had shown me that morning.

"Mornin'." He nodded curtly. I followed him as he walked around to the other side of the truck, opened the door, and removed a wooden toolbox. He slammed the door with a thundering *bang*. "Do you need something?" he asked pointedly.

"Are you John Holbrock?" My voice was shakier than I would have liked.

"I am."

"Brian told me you might be able to find a shirt in the attic. I need a shirt for my son. We're new here." I offered a weak grin.

"Don' have any boys' clothes that I know of." He walked around to the tailgate, opened it, and pulled out several long boards.

I sighed. "Well, I guess he can go without."

John shook his head as he leaned the boards against the bed of the truck. "The ladies won' let 'im. It's not proper to run about half naked."

"What do you mean? Men and boys walk around without shirts at the pool all the time."

"This isn't the pool." He hoisted the boards to his shoulder, balancing them with one hand. With his other hand, he reached down to pick up the handle of the toolbox. Then he started for the house.

I followed him. "But you know what I mean. I

guess back years ago when Mrs. McGregor was young, it was probably improper, but—"

"It's not her," he interrupted in a sour voice. "It's the *other* old ladies. The Double P's. They won't let us work without shirts, because it was improper in the eighteenth century. I s'pose they're old enough to remember, heh, heh." His hoarse laugh turned into a cough, but his steady pace never slowed.

I had to struggle to keep up with him. "Well, maybe my son could wear a man's shirt, just for today. Do you think you might have any of those?"

"Don' know."

I was getting really exasperated by his attitude. "Could you look? When you have time, that is."

He shook his head. "Don' have keys to the attic."

"Well, if I get keys from someone, could you—"

"No. I'm late to set up my demonstration." He bowed his head in a meaningless gesture of civility before turning abruptly away from me, taking the path around the house instead of through it.

I made an ugly face at his back and charged after him, rounding the corner just in time to run smack into Brian. I stumbled backward, slipping on the wet grass, but eventually managed to regain my balance without falling this time.

He grinned. "We've got to stop meeting like this."

Before I could think of a cute answer, he had turned to John. "Can I give you a hand with the lumber?"

"I can manage. Don' you need to tend your precious fire?"

Brian beamed at me. "I've got an assistant today.

He can keep watch over the fire while I help you unload. What else needs to come out of the truck?"

"I'll get it," John said flatly, with a quick, almost nervous glance toward the parking lot. He dropped the load of boards. "You take these." Without another word, he disappeared around the side of the building.

Was John hiding something in his truck? I turned to Brian. "Boy, you'd think you suggested driving the truck off a cliff, rather than helping him with it."

"Don't mind him," Brian said gently. "He's holding a grudge against a great many of us at the moment, but I think it will pass if we just give it time."

So John might have taken the Washington notes not only for their resale value but also to get revenge. I fought the urge to follow him back to his truck. If he had taken the notes, he surely would have moved them somewhere else by now.

I questioned Brian instead. Though I probably should have asked why John was mad, it seemed like a nosy question, and I didn't want Brian to think I was one of those gossipy types. "If he's mad at you, why does he still come to volunteer? And why is he so protective of his truck?"

Brian's mouth set in a grim line. "He doesn't want any of us near the truck because somebody wrote a nasty accusation on his windshield not so long ago. He was pretty mad at all of us, and he didn't come back for quite a while. But I guess he missed the place. And. . ." Brian lowered his voice and looked around to be sure we were alone before continuing. "I don't think he's welcome at most of the other sites in this area."

I really needed to hear the story behind the theft

allegations. But something about the somber expression on Brian's face told me it would be a waste of time to ask him. He was not going to spread gossip.

So I would have to find someone who would.

## 9

"What happened to all my red, white, and blue bunting?" Ann Bleckenstrauss moaned as she walked around the yard with a dazed expression on her face. "And the balloons are all gone."

I remembered Paula's dexterity with her hat pin and realized she'd probably had quite a bit of practice. "How many balloons did you have?" I asked with a sympathetic smile.

"A package. Three dozen, I think." She pouted, the lines of her mouth pulled down in a line that matched the droop of the ribbons on her cap. "I thought some of them might pop before we opened since I put them up so early, but all of them?"

"And you said you had bunting up, too? That certainly didn't pop. Someone must have taken it down." I let my gaze stray toward the kitchen.

Okay, so it wasn't very nice of me to stir up the long-simmering feud between the "house ladies" and the "actors in the yard," but I had a feeling this would get Ann started talking.

"It was those two." Ann stared at the brick kitchen building with cross-eyed fury. "I'm surprised they didn't throw away everything on the bake sale table because we used the wrong color sugar or baked cookies on a period-incorrect pan." She stepped over to the baked goods and touched several of the plates as if to reassure herself that they were still there.

An older man and woman, visitors obviously, stepped

out of the house arm in arm. Though they strolled slowly to enjoy the beautiful morning, their eyes were ultimately focused on a Boston cream pie at the end of the bake table.

Ann plopped into a chair behind the cash box.

"I can help you here, if you'd like," I offered.

"That would be lovely."

"You're selling the food on this table and raffle tickets to win the baskets on that table?"

"Yes."

I glanced at the Boston-cream-pie couple. They had paused to examine a flowering plant and probably wouldn't reach us for another minute or two. "I could see where balloons might be a problem, but why would anyone take down your bunting?"

Ann sighed. "Paula thinks we have too much red, white, and blue. But we're the 1776 House. People expect lots of it. They come to hear about George Washington, not Josiah Barnswallow." She waved toward the kitchen. "None of those *reenactors* understand."

"Understand?"

"The public come to see the stars. They know only a few names, a few numbers. George Washington. Seventeen seventy-six. If we publicize our connection with those names, people come to see us. We should be working in partnership with the big groups, like the Daughters of the American Patriots. If we don't associate with big names, the people don't care. They don't come. And then we have to close down." She nodded toward Paula, who was coming out of the kitchen with a tall canister of something hot. "So all their hard work is for nothing. Would you like to buy a brownie?"

I blinked at the sudden change of subject and was about to answer that I didn't usually eat dessert at this hour of the morning, when I realized that Ann had addressed her last comment not to me but to a young girl whose Pippi Longstocking pigtails barely reached the top of the table. The girl nodded and held out a quarter.

A boy next to her held out his own quarter and pointed at a tray of chocolate cupcakes covered with colored candies shaped like dinosaurs. I was fairly certain they were not period correct. But they did sell well.

Even without balloons, the raffle and bake sale attracted enough attention to keep us busy throughout the rest of the morning, so I did not have the opportunity to ask Ann about John or the closer connection she sought with the Daughters of the American Patriots. Most of my attention was consumed with money and frosting. I was vaguely aware that John was sawing and filing and pounding with various tools on the other side of the yard, and I thought Paula was probably dipping candles, although it really looked more like she was fishing.

At one point, Brian walked out of the blacksmith shop, winked at me, bought a bag of cookies from Ann, and handed the bag to a group of kids watching John's demonstration. Then he joined the carpentry demonstration for a while, but I couldn't really see what they were doing.

I dropped three cupcakes, frosting side down, on the grass. In later generations, when archaeologists find the remains of the dinosaur candies, they might come to question George Washington's mental state as he prepared for the Battle of the Brandywine.

Ann left to give house tours, so the responsibility for peddling sugar rested solely on my shoulders for about half an hour. Then the crowd began to thin and John stopped working, stood up straight, and rubbed his back. Patty stepped out of the kitchen and marched across the yard with her usual deliberate gait, probably headed for the bathroom in the house. But she stopped suddenly in front of John.

"Why don't you sit down for a while," she suggested, pointing to the chair next to me at the bake table. "You can help Karen and rest at the same time."

"And eat brownies." I held up a big square, wrapped in plastic and tied with period-incorrect ribbon.

A genuine smile lit his face. "Now that's the best idea I've heard all day."

"Steak pie should be about ready." Patty nodded toward the kitchen. "I'll bring you both a piece when it is."

He looked as if he was about to refuse but then looked at the chair and nodded. "That'd be great."

"So what are you making over there?" I asked John between bites a few minutes later.

"A new table for the kitchen." He pulled a checked handkerchief from his pocket and wiped his brow. "Heavier work than I've done in some time. I us'ally make boxes and small trunks these days."

"What do you do with them?" I couldn't remember seeing any wooden boxes for sale in the gift shop. "Sell them here?"

"Oh no. The visitors we get here aren't interested in detailed reproductions. My pieces are all based on originals, made completely with hand tools, and finished with period oils." He grinned. "They cost a little more than the made-in-China garbage they sell in the gift shop."

"So who's willing to pay for these reproductions?" I hoped my interest sounded casual. "Is there a collector's market?"

He chewed thoughtfully and then swallowed. "There are some collectors, I guess. I sell mostly to reenactors who are willing to put forth the effort to create a quality impression."

"So they don't necessarily want original pieces, but good reproductions."

He nodded. "Most of 'em, yeah. Can't afford the originals."

"So who has all the originals?"

"Prob'ly collectors, like you said. Small museums. And regular people who don't realize that Aunt Agatha's papers in the attic are stored in an original eighteenth-century black walnut box."

"Well, how would people know something was that old?" I set down my plate and glanced around, hoping no one would come to interrupt us.

He pursed his lips to the side for a moment. "You can tell by the style of construction and the finish, and by the patina on the wood. To get really accurate, they might do a dendo."

"A what?"

"Dendochronology." He waved toward a large oak on the side of the house. "Study the growth pattern of the tree rings in the wood. When compared with known samples, you get a pretty accurate read."

I wished I could take notes. "What about carbon 14 dating?"

"The problem with radiocarbon dating is that you have to burn up a piece of the artifact you're trying to date."

"So if you prove something is authentic, is it worth a lot more?"

He looked at me as if that was a stupid question.

"Was that a stupid question?"

He held up two fingers. "That makes two now."

I laughed. "Okay. So have you ever discovered a box, like an aunt's box that someone had in their attic, and you got it from them cheap and then discovered you could sell it for lots of money?"

His light mood vanished. He glowered at me for a moment. "Wouldn' be any of your business if I had." Then he turned away and stared at the house.

Long minutes passed during which neither of us said anything except to intermittent bake sale and raffle customers. After a few more minutes, John simply stood and walked back to his carpentry display. I found myself staring at the back of the house just as John had done, waiting for Ann to come back out. Since John wouldn't tell me any more about himself, I hoped she might instead.

But when Ann appeared, it wasn't John she wanted to talk about. "I was right," she gushed as she stashed her period-incorrect faux designer handbag underneath the chair. "Eileen saw Paula Lowell popping balloons out here this morning. She probably took down the bunting, too—it was all designed to highlight our fund-raiser. We probably won't sell enough raffle tickets to help pay for the storm damage to the roof. Blast that woman. Always thinks she knows what's best."

"So you think it was just Paula? Or do you think Patty helped?" I wanted to get an idea of how often they worked together.

"Does it matter? They always defend one another. If Patty didn't help, she would still give me a twenty-minute lecture on why her sister did the right thing." Ann collapsed into the chair and cast a disparaging eye over the trays of cupcakes and pies still remaining on the table. "It's going to be harder to sell this stuff as the afternoon wears on. We'd better start discounting it."

I reached for an extremely ugly gray cake. It was dusted with what I assumed was powdered sugar but what really looked like dust.

"Wait a minute." Ann grabbed my arm.

The cake was probably hers. I wondered if I had inadvertently made the comment about dust aloud.

"You've been out here all day, haven't you?" she asked.

I nodded. "I guess so."

She patted my arm. "Well, you've done enough, then. Why don't you take a tray of cookies around to the volunteers and see if any of them would like one, and then find something else to do for the rest of the afternoon?"

"Okay." Until she'd said something, I hadn't realized just how tired I was of selling desserts. I loaded a plate with cookies and brownies, wondering which ones might be Brian's favorites. I included M&M cookies for Evan and peanut butter bars for Alicia, too.

Patty had apparently taken a break from her candle-making demonstration, and John pointedly looked away when I held up the cookie tray. So I decided to offer the cookies to the guys in the blacksmith shop. It took my eyes a moment to adjust to the dim light after the bright sunlight outside. A family was just thanking Brian and heading for the door, so I smashed myself against the wall to give them room to pass by. The bricks felt cool against my back. I tried to figure out whether the heat in my skin was due to sunburn or the nervous fit of butterflies in my stomach at the thought of asking Brian out. I really didn't even want to now, but almost for that very reason, I felt as if I had to. If I could somehow do it, just ask one guy on a casual date, then I would prove to myself that I had moved beyond Jeff. That I had healed.

As I stepped toward the forge, I tripped on a loose brick. Though I managed to keep hold of the tray, at least half of the cookies flew forward, hurtling off the edge in a suicidal rush to kingdom crumb.

I looked at the M&M's scattered on the dirty bricks. "Oh, Evan, I'm so sorry. Those were your favorites."

Evan smiled as he looked up from a piece of iron he was holding with tongs. "That's okay, Mom. I'm not hungry."

I held out the tray toward Brian. "Would you like one of the survivors?"

"Did you make them?"

I shook my head. "I didn't even know there was a bake sale today."

He smiled. "In that case, I think I'll pass."

*So he would have taken one if I had made it?* My heart warmed at the thought until I realized he probably would have eaten one just to be polite. Still, there was that smile.

I realized I was staring at him, probably with my mouth open. I immediately dropped my gaze to the floor. "We need that dog in here this week to clean up the crumbs."

There was a laugh—I had made Brian laugh again. I looked up to see that Evan was focused on his iron creation, and Brian was focused on me.

"We should recruit that dog as a volunteer to liven things up around here," he suggested, still grinning.

Much as I hated to ruin his mood, I had to test him. He was still a suspect. "The ladies in the house would probably welcome him if we pretended he was *George Washington's* dog." I held my breath. Would he laugh, or would the mere mention of Washington bring a frown to his face?

He paused as if considering the idea. "Washington probably had a number of dogs. We might be able to pass him off."

I smiled.

"But since we don't have that Washington craziness to worry about anymore, it's probably better if we don't even mention the name." He shook his head sadly. "I'm sure the ladies in the house weren't happy to take down the display."

He seemed actually sorry.

*Or* he was a good actor. I could almost hear Dave's voice in my head. *"Never discount a suspect. Some of the best actors in the world never set foot on a stage."*

"Have you checked to see if anyone in the house wants a cookie?" Brian nodded toward the tray that I forgot I was still holding.

"Oh no, not yet," I admitted with reluctance. "I

haven't asked Patty, either."

Brian smiled. "You can probably skip her. She's already supplied with the best."

So he preferred Patty's steak pie to my cookies. I turned and left without another word. My steps slowed as I crossed the yard. They weren't really my cookies.

I was an excellent baker.

Maybe I wasn't a super career woman, but I was pretty good in the baking-cupcakes-for-birthdays, patching jeans, and finding-props-for-shoe-box-dioramas department. For a long time, that was all I thought I had to be good at.

Apparently Jeff thought I should have been good at putting on makeup and prancing around in tight capri pants and high-heeled sandals.

I looked down at my dowdy apron and long skirt.

Then, with a sigh, I looked up at the windows of the second story of the house.

I was not supposed to be feeling sorry for myself. I was not supposed to be thinking about my ex-husband or possible future boyfriend. The only man with whom I was supposed to be concerned wore false teeth, chopped down cherry trees, and had been dead for more than two hundred years.

*What happened to your notes, George?* I asked silently. The house didn't answer, so I turned and headed back toward the kitchen to see if someone there would.

## 10

As Evan walked into the smoky, dark colonial kitchen, he glared at his sister, who sat on a trunk near the window. "Why are you wearing my bathrobe?"

"You never wear it," Alicia answered without even looking up from the hem of the apron she was sewing.

"That was Evan's bathrobe you cut up?" I had the feeling I was about three steps behind my children in comprehending the situation, but I figured my bewilderment was due to excess smoke inhalation. Baking in the colonial kitchen seemed to involve cooking myself as much as any actual food. It seemed like I had spent most of the last hour in front of the fire, shoveling coals onto bake kettles under Patty's guidance, and my hands and face felt sunburned.

I looked at Alicia's outfit and could now conjure up vague memories of Evan opening a Christmas box from his grandmother. Alicia was right in saying that he hadn't worn the bathrobe, but she needed to be upbraided for taking it without permission nevertheless, especially since I had barely said a word about her cutting up my favorite sheets. I directed a stern motherly gaze at her. "You should have asked him before you cut up his belongings."

She shrugged, still focused on her sewing. "He can have it back anyway. It's polyester. I need something made of—"

I waved my hand in front of her face to get her attention. "It's also ruined, Alicia. You had no right to ruin your brother's property."

She scowled. "Well, he had no right to read my diary to his friends."

I spun around to face him. "Evan! When did you—"

"That was the day you yelled at me for flushing his LEGOs down the toilet," Alicia added to clarify the situation.

I turned back to her. "You flushed. . ." Then I stopped. If I had yelled at her for it, I must have known about it. "LEGOs could really mess up the plumbing."

"Hush now, no more talk of LEGOs." Patty grinned. "We've guests arriving."

Evan disappeared out the back door as the same family I saw leaving the blacksmith shop now made their way into the kitchen.

"But it's not my fault the milk spilled!" Alicia suddenly wailed in an earsplitting stage voice. She fell to her knees at Patty's feet. "Please don't have me executed."

Since the last misbehavior that I remembered involved bathrobes, I was completely lost. And in my own defense, I have to say that I have never once threatened to kill her, although the sight of my bed-sheets in tatters might have driven me to it had I not needed her cooperation so badly.

Patty immediately suppressed a grin and addressed Alicia in a stern voice. "Calm yourself, girl, and get back to work. I know you were accused of theft for letting the cow kick over the milk pail back in England, but the master here is liable to forgive you, if you don't burn his dinner."

"I was so frightened!" Alicia held up her trembling hands for the benefit of the visitors. "When they took me to court and stood me before the judge, I could see the gallows in front of me."

I was very glad Evan had left, because his howls of laughter would really undercut Alicia's dramatic moment here.

"But then. . ." Alicia paused theatrically. "I remembered that if I could prove I could read, they would change my sentence. I asked for a Bible and read a passage. So instead of executing me, the judge sent me to America." She bowed her head, and I wondered whether we were supposed to applaud.

Patty prodded her on the shoulder. "Well, now you're here, and you have to do my bidding for the next seven years until your indenture is up."

Alicia looked up with a light of hope shining in her immigrant eyes. "Yes, and then the master will have to give me my freedom dues, which includes—"

"What's that burning smell?" one of the visitors asked. He was not much younger than Evan. I gave him credit for not laughing at Alicia's melodramatic performance.

"Something in the fire, probably," his dad said, shushing him.

"You've burned the master's dinner," I teased Alicia.

Patty wrinkled her nose thoughtfully as she stepped closer to the fire. "Actually, I believe it's the master's shortbread that is burning."

I ran around the worktable, pushed in front of Patty, and started fumbling through all the iron implements to find something to lift the lid off the bake kettle. Smoke poured from inside, and the smell of burnt sugar assailed my nose.

"Rats." I poked at the charred mass. Brian was not going to be impressed with my baking this time.

"We're having rat again?" a male voice boomed out behind me. "That's the third time this week."

I turned around to see Brian standing in the doorway with an exaggerated frown on his face.

Patty shook a wooden spoon at him accusingly. "And you'll not complain, either, unless you want mud for your dinner."

"What's the master have for his table?" Brian asked. He looked so sullen, so much like a resentful servant, I nearly shivered. He was indeed a good actor. Just as Dave had warned.

Patty launched into her recitation of the day's cooking activities, and I found myself sneaking glances at Brian. The frown made him look dark and forbidding. Like the hero on the cover of a grocery store novel, handsome but unreal.

I realized he looked unreal because I didn't really think he was dark and forbidding. He was actually a very nice guy, a guy who liked to teach kids and help others. He was the perfect guy to ask on a date, because if he said no, he would be sure to do it in a nice way.

"What are you staring at?" Patty poked me with her spoon. "Get that burned mess out of here before the foul miasmic vapors make us all take to our beds." She winked at me and glanced meaningfully at Brian.

So I had probably been staring at Brian with some sort of vacant, drooling expression, like a woman staring at the cover of a romance novel.

Earlier she had warned me that the pan I'd chosen might be difficult to remove from the bake kettle before it cooled, so I just hauled the whole smoldering mess outside with the pot lifter before I could embarrass myself further.

I set the kettle down on the grass in the yard and watched the smoke rise from the charred remains of the dish I had hoped to use to impress Brian. As sweat dripped down the side of my face, I wiped it away with the back of my hand.

"Do you need help with that?" Brian's voice sounded behind me.

"No." As I turned around, I realized I had probably just smeared soot all over my face. I wiped my hands on my apron. "Well, actually, I'm not sure how to get the pan out of there." I nodded toward the kettle.

He bent down. "If you tilt it to the side, you have room to fit your hand in." He wrapped a handkerchief around his hand several times and extracted the smoking pan from the kettle. Then he set the pan on the grass.

"I really made a mess of it."

"Happens all the time. The inside is probably still good." He took a knife from his pocket and tried to pry a piece out of the middle.

I squeezed my eyes shut and braced myself for the worst, not really sure what that might be. "Would-you-like-to-come-over-for-dinner-sometime?"

"What?"

I opened my eyes just enough to see that Brian looked very confused, as if he'd just been given one of Brittany's cryptic phone messages. I took a deep breath and forced myself to speak slowly. "If I promise not to burn the food, would you be willing to come over for dinner one night?" I fought the urge to close my eyes again and looked at him with what was probably a pathetic pleading expression.

This time he was the one who closed his eyes, but only for a second. It was a blink of surprise. "You mean, like on a—"

"Like to eat dinner." I cut him off before he could say the word "date," because it didn't seem as though he was any more eager to say it than I was to hear it. "You know. You've got to eat. Even if you're busy." I offered a lame smile.

"Well, yeah. Sure." He still looked a little disconcerted but was recovering nicely. "When?"

"When?" I think my mouth probably fell open again. I hadn't thought that far ahead. All my nervous energy was focused on asking him. I had given no thought whatsoever to the event itself. When should he come over? What would I cook?

"I have youth group on Sunday nights and meetings lots of times on Tuesdays, but Wednesdays are usually good," he offered.

"Wednesdays." I was now behaving like a parrot, simply repeating his words. Before I started looking around for a cracker, I made myself think. Wednesday was the night Jeff took the kids out for dinner. If Brian came over, we would be alone. Like on a real date. Was this a good thing? "Um, sure. This Wednesday?" Ooh, bad idea. Now I looked desperate.

But perhaps desperation appealed to him. Because he smiled and said, "Yeah, that'd be great."

A great bubbly feeling rose up inside me. It was like picking up a bottle of soda that's so old you assume it's flat, but when you shake it just to be sure, you find that there is still plenty of fizz left.

I really did it. I asked him out. And he said yes.

Mrs. McGregor stepped out of the house and marched across the yard toward Brian with a frown furrowing her forehead. "I really think the Property Committee is letting the grass get too long," she announced in a loud voice. "And the trees at the front of the house have needed pruning since last year."

The bubbles popped. I wasn't here to ask Brian over for dinner. I was here to work for *her*. She was paying me to find a thief. Instead, all I had done was sell cookies, burn food, and ask one of the suspects on a date by misleading him about my nonexistent interest in history.

I dumped the charred shortbread into the grass and started scraping the pan, as if I could physically scrape away the mounting guilt.

Brian stood with a sigh and squared off to face Mrs. McGregor. "If you don't like the yard maintenance schedule, I suggest you come to one of the Property Committee meetings."

She planted her hands on her hips, looking much more like a twentieth-century feminist than an eighteenth-century tour guide. "I don't need to come to a meeting. Anyone can see the problem."

"Come to the meeting, next Tuesday, 7:00 p.m." Brian said flatly. "I'm not going to discuss this now, in front of guests."

Before I could determine whether he considered me a guest, he had started back toward the blacksmith shop.

It was getting late, and I might not see him again. Until Wednesday.

⁓

Jeff pulled up the driveway in a new green convertible that looked as if it should have been driven in one of those TV shows in Southern California. A convertible. A new car. This from the man who insisted that the court-ordered child support was more than he could afford.

"Is this your car?" Alicia squealed as she ran out the door to greet him.

"Linda thought we needed something more fun," he said in a low voice as he hugged her. I'm sure he was hoping I hadn't heard that.

"You haven't hidden her in the trunk or anything, have you?" I asked as I walked out behind Alicia.

"Who?"

"You know. She's not supposed to be with you on these visits. The judge agreed that—"

"Yeah, yeah, yeah." Jeff made a face at me and lowered his sunglasses to offer a conspiratorial wink over my shoulder to Evan. "I thought we'd go to a drive-in tonight—whaddya think, guys?"

"A drive-in?" I tried to make my voice heard over the kids' chorus of glee. "Where?"

"We don't have to tell you, do we?" Jeff pushed his sunglasses back into place. "As long as we're back by 9:00."

"Have fun, then. I hope it doesn't rain. I'm sure that's not good for the leather interior. And watch out for mosquitoes. And bees."

Jeff made an obnoxious slurping noise. "There she goes again. Your mother just sucking the fun out of everything."

I smiled. "I try." Then I turned back toward the house so he wouldn't see me fume.

A convertible. Because they "*needed something more fun*." It hadn't been enough fun to simply trade in his life for a new one—now he needed a new car, too. And the kids thought it was wonderful and exciting, just like everything else their father did.

By the time I stepped back into the house, I was seeing red. I glanced at my reflection in the hall mirror, half expecting it to show smoke coming from my ears. "C'mon, Tara!" I grabbed the dog's leash from the hook in the pantry. "We need a walk."

Usually she would pull me down the street. But this time, I was the one pulling her. She would have to hustle along, forgoing all sniffing opportunities until I decided it really didn't matter that Jeff had a new car. Until Jeff didn't matter at all. It would be a long walk.

But I really didn't have all that much time. I needed to get dinner together. And while I should have been happy about the reason I was cooking a gourmet meal instead of microwaving a TV dinner, I was too nervous to be anything approaching happy. Yes, Brian was ten times better-looking than Jeff, but he probably just accepted my offer because he felt sorry for me. I didn't know what to wear, whether to put on makeup, what music to play, what to say, how to act—the list was endless.

The one thing I did not have to worry about

was the dinner itself. With a modern kitchen at my disposal, I was a pretty good cook.

Tara was panting heavily by the time I turned back onto my own street. I was trying to remember what temperature to preheat the oven.

"Hi, Karen!" My neighbor—now I remembered her name was Amy—waved from the front porch, where she was sitting blowing bubbles with her young daughter, a blond, curly-headed cherub of about three.

I waved back with a quick "Hi" and was ready to head for my own porch, but Tara had other ideas. She yanked me toward Amy's yard with sudden fury.

Amy laughed as Tara sniffed around her knees. "We picked up chicken nuggets on the way home." She held up a white paper bag. "Can your dog have one?"

"Sure."

"After all that walking, you probably both need the energy!"

"I, uh, oh yeah, maybe."

She gave me a wistful smile. "I really admire the way you get out and walk so regularly. They say walking is the best form of exercise."

"Well, it's a way of killing two birds with one stone." I looked toward my house, trying to will the dog away from the bag of chicken nuggets.

My willpower wasn't very effective. Tara kept nuzzling Amy's legs until at last Amy pulled out the bag again. She held it up. "You know, we really don't need to eat the rest of these. Can she have them?"

"I guess."

"I didn't intend to buy them, but when we walked

by the carryout, they smelled so good." She wrapped her arm around her daughter's shoulder. "Didn't they, pumpkin?"

"French fries!" the girl cried gleefully, flinging her arm up into the air and spraying sticky bubble solution in my face.

Amy chuckled as she fed chicken to the grateful dog. "Yes, we had French fries, too. I really need to be out walking to work off those calories! But I just can't seem to get started. I guess I need a partner."

"That's probably a good idea, at least to get going regularly," I agreed, my attention wandering back to my house. I needed to peel the potatoes and—

"Well, don't let us keep you any longer." Amy smiled cheerfully as she wadded up the empty carryout bag.

"Oh, okay." I had probably just been very rude in my obvious haste to get away. "See you later." I hoped the dog would pull me away to make the awkward parting moment a little less awkward. But instead she buried her nose in the ground, looking for crumbs, and I had to drag her away.

"It was nice talking to you."

"Yeah, real nice." I tried to make it look as though I wasn't having to use every muscle in my body to drag the dog back to our house. "C'mon," I whispered to the stubborn canine. "Two extra rawhide treats if you hurry home."

She didn't exactly hurry, but she did come along well enough that I decided she was entitled to one rawhide treat. I flipped on the oven to preheat and reached for the box of dog treats in the top cabinet, pulling the whole super-shoppers-club-sized box down on my head. Slews of gravy-basted rawhide chips showered onto the floor. The dog managed to snatch up at least seven of them before I pulled her out into the backyard.

As I shoved the rest back into the box, I grimaced at the weird smell and plastic texture. Who would have ever thought of these things as edible, let alone a "treat"? Well, I guess a dog would. Creatures that sniff one another in greeting obviously have some different standards. I held one of the chips up to the light. Rawhide was hide, the skin of steer, probably. Hard leather. If I soaked my leather jacket in gravy and put it in the oven for several days, it would probably look like this. The dog would be clawing at the closet door to get it.

As I thought of Tara gleefully heading out into the yard with her treats, I also remembered the dog at the 1776 House dashing through the yard with a stolen cake.

The Washington notes had been written on a scrap of leather, hadn't they? Was it possible that the thief had four legs and a tail?

I pondered the possibility while I closed the box of rawhide treats and made room for them on a lower shelf.

## 11

Sometime during the day, the gray strands in my hair had multiplied. I was getting old. Frumpy. Unattractive.

In half an hour, I would have my first date in over fifteen years, and I would come to the door looking like my mother.

It was too late to do much of anything with my hair, which is so short that I rarely even bother to comb it. I tried to curl it, but this made me look even more like my mother. I gave up and slicked it back with some mousse.

My hands shook as I put on eyeliner, so one eye came out looking bigger than the other. I smeared mascara all over my eyelid. Then I had to find some makeup remover and start over.

The timer in the kitchen buzzed, telling me that the pork tenderloin was done. But it would have to wait. If I went downstairs with eyes like a rabid raccoon, the sight might send Brian running for the hills. It took a lot longer to wipe off the eye makeup than it had to put it on. Then I steadied my hand and prepared to start over.

The doorbell rang.

The dog let out a succession of outraged barks as I dropped the eyeliner and ran to the window. Of course, I couldn't see the front porch because of the roof, so it was a pointless exercise. But since I could see a white pickup truck parked on the street, I guessed that the doorbell was probably Brian and not a Girl Scout coming to collect cookie money.

I forced myself to breathe. This was just dinner. He had to eat, and he was here to eat. We could talk about the weather and maybe the Orioles—wait, baseball season was over, wasn't it? I could fake my way through a discussion of baseball because Dave played in high school, but I didn't think I could manage football. What else did guys talk about?

The doorbell rang again. I picked at my hair one last time and then ran downstairs, arriving breathless and flinging open the door with such force that it made a weird sucking noise.

Then we both laughed. Seeing Brian dressed in regular clothes was not as big a shock as I had thought it might be. With long hair pulled back, he still looked something like a pirate, even wearing a decidedly unpirateish blue pullover sweater.

When I opened the screen door to let him in, the dog immediately launched herself at him, barking like a fiend. I grabbed her collar and hauled her back inside as I offered Brian an apologetic smile. "I'm sorry. She takes her job as guard dog too seriously. She'll be fine once you get in the house."

But she wasn't any better. She barked and leaped at Brian as if he were an army of invading supercats.

"Maybe she got a bad chicken nugget or something," I suggested as I dragged Tara toward the patio door. Once I had pushed her out into the backyard and closed the door, I turned back to face Brian. Well, now at least in addition to the weather we could talk about mad dogs.

He held out a small green plant with long droopy leaves in a plain terra-cotta pot. "I brought you some sorrel."

Sorrel? Well, it was better than getting a bouquet of flowers left over from someone's funeral (which Dave gave to my mother one year), or even the half-dead discounted flowers Jeff would occasionally bring me. But it wasn't terribly attractive. "Thanks," I said as I reached for the plant, wondering how to work this into the mad-dog conversation.

An apologetic smile lit his features. "You have no idea what it is, do you? I'm sorry. Patty was so happy to have some, I thought you might like it, too."

He was equating me with the motherly Patty? Ouch.

"Since you like eighteenth-century cooking so much," he continued. "It's an herb that used to be very popular. Now it's hard to find. We had some in the garden at the House years ago, but it was overrun by a patch of horseradish. Then I found some out there yesterday, so I thought you might like it."

"I—I do," I said in a thoroughly unconvincing manner.

"It doesn't keep dried, so it has to be used fresh."

I looked at the pot stupidly. "That's good to know."

"It has a really unique taste. Here, try it." Brian reached over, broke off a small leaf, and held it to my mouth. The touch of his fingers left a tingling sensation on my lips that I was fairly certain had nothing to do with the herb. But he was right. It did have a wonderful tangy taste.

"Hey, that is neat. Thank you." This time I sounded genuine.

He beamed. "I knew you would appreciate it. Once you found out what it was. So now when you see it in a recipe, you'll have it."

"Uh, yeah." The happy tingling sensation abruptly vanished as I remembered that I had brought Brian in under false pretenses. If he liked me at all, it was because he thought I was interested in eighteenth-century life, just as he was. He didn't know I was just there to get paid and that I did not spend my spare time poring over colonial cookbooks.

His nose wrinkled as if he were about to sneeze. "Is something burning?" he asked, looking around.

I shoved the sorrel back into his hands and ran into the kitchen, a feeling of horror gripping me as I read the clock on the stove. The pork and potatoes should have come out of the oven at least half an hour ago. My fears were confirmed as I opened the oven door and saw blackened potatoes and pork tenderloin that bore far too much resemblance to the rawhide strips that Tara had overdosed on earlier. The only thing left of dinner now was the salad.

"Are you by any chance a vegetarian?" I asked Brian as he stepped into the kitchen.

He laughed. "As a matter of fact, I was just thinking that it was time to cut down on meat and potatoes. I need to drop a few pounds."

"No, you don't," I said quickly. He looked awfully good just the way he was. "We still have dessert. I can't burn that. It's in the refrigerator with the salad." I gestured toward the fridge, but I was still looking at

Brian, thinking that the blue of his sweater made his eyes look even deeper than usual. Ahem. I had to stop looking at Brian so that I could salvage something of dinner.

"Chicken or shrimp?" I asked over my shoulder as I began to rummage through the freezer.

"For?"

"To add to the salad. And don't tell me it doesn't matter because I really get tired of making dinner decisions."

"Can I say 'whichever is easiest'?" he asked. "I didn't come over to make you work."

"Yes, you can." As I pulled a package of chicken tenders from the freezer, I bit back the urge to ask why he *had* come over. He probably came over to share the sorrel with me and talk about eighteenth-century ironwork.

"Would you like to watch TV or something?" I offered. "It won't take me long to cook this up."

"I'd rather stay in here and talk with you, if that's okay."

"Sure." I smiled uneasily. *Did they have baseball in the eighteenth century?* Well, they definitely had weather, so that topic remained safe. I dumped the chicken in a skillet. "Should I add some sorrel to this, do you think?"

Brian leaned back against the counter near me. "That would be good, but I think you'd better give the plant a chance to get a bit bigger before you start stripping the leaves."

"Oh. Yeah." I stirred the chicken in silence, trying to think up some remarkable aspect of the weather.

But I couldn't remember if it had been warm or cold, sunny or rainy that day. I just kept thinking that this was the first time a man would be sitting down in my kitchen. Jeff had come over before, but I never let him stay long enough to sit down.

What could I say to him? If I started asking questions about the 1776 House, he might soon realize that it was work, and not interest, that brought me there. And besides, I didn't want to talk about work.

"Have you known Patty and Paula long?" Brian asked.

I dropped the spatula into the pan. "Patty and Paula?" Was he already suspicious? "No longer than I've known you," I answered warily.

"Really? I thought you were old friends the way Patty took Alicia under her wing and you started coming so regularly. I heard you tell Patty you would see her next week," he added quickly, coloring a bit as if embarrassed to admit he had been eavesdropping.

I was pleased he found my conversations worth listening to. But rather than bask in the glow of joy over this apparent sign of interest, I decided that since he brought up the subject, I really had to follow up to see what I could learn. "Patty and Paula seem like wonderful women. Really committed to teaching history."

He laughed. "Yeah, I think they're really committed to everything they do. Nothing halfway done."

So if Paula wanted an authentic site with the notes out of the way, she wouldn't hesitate to steal them? I forced a laugh. "You make them sound almost ruthless."

He grimaced. "Well, I didn't mean to go that far. Just determined, then."

"Like if they wanted something accomplished, nothing could stand in their way?"

A smile lit his features, and he laughed. "Yeah. When they decided I wasn't eating enough, Patty started sending me home with so much extra food I had to rent freezer space."

I smiled as I let out a sigh of relief. Paula was looking more and more like the culprit, which meant Brian would be off the hook.

---

"Sorry about the dessert," I apologized again as I looked at the coffee mugs sitting on the otherwise empty table. We were supposed to be eating chocolate mousse at this point, but since I dropped the bowl while pulling it out of the refrigerator, only the dog had been able to get a taste of it before I shooed her away. Now the floor was clean, but both Brian and I had sticky flecks of chocolate on the legs of our pants. "I'd be happy to pay for dry cleaning if—"

He put his hand over mine. "Stop." His voice was calm and low, as if he were trying to talk a scared cat down out of a tree. "I want you to stop apologizing for everything. This has been a terrific dinner, and stop trying to tell me that it wasn't."

I looked down at my lap, embarrassed at the sensation of almost being chastised, and also by the realization that the warmth of Brian's hand on my own was making me blush. It was no doubt meant to be a soothing gesture. But I felt like a giddy schoolgirl with a crush.

"You seem really jumpy tonight."

"I've been nervous," I admitted. "I haven't had a da—anyone over for dinner in so many years. I wanted everything to be perfect." Even though I stopped myself before I said the *d* word, I had come too close.

He frowned and moved his hand away to fiddle with the handle of his coffee mug. Then his expression brightened. "It really hasn't been years since you had *anyone* over to dinner. You've got five chairs at this table."

I tried to match his light tone, but a lump rose in my throat. "The kids have had friends over." But until now I had never thought of the fact that I had not. I had not invited anyone to this house from the day we signed the lease.

"And you make your friends eat outside?" His voice was teasing, but the sincere expression in his eyes said that he was listening, really listening, if I wanted to talk.

"I guess I don't have time to invite anyone over." I wouldn't even know whom to invite. Everyone else was married, and they all did things with other couples. Like Jeff and Linda.

"We all get busy." He paused, and when he spoke again, his tone grew very soft. "But sometimes that busyness is a deliberate way to avoid things."

"You sound like one of those self-help people." I looked away, the lump in my throat getting bigger all the time. I realized now that I might have deliberately chosen not to invite anyone inside.

To my surprise, he laughed. "I do sound like a counselor or something. I guess I'm just repeating what my pastor has said to me so many times."

"So what are you avoiding?" Yeah, I shouldn't have said that. I didn't know him well enough. But he started it.

"If I talk about it, I won't be doing a very good job of avoiding it, will I?" His tone was not quite as confident as before. I had struck a nerve.

"Chicken," I accused.

"Oh, most definitely." He said this more to himself than to me.

So now I was making him as nervous as he had made me. What a wonderful date this was turning out to be. I glanced around, desperate for a new topic of conversation. "So, uh, nice weather we're having."

He winced. "Am I that bad?"

"Not you. Me." I was boring. I had no life, nothing to talk about. Here was someone who knew next to nothing about me. I could have told him almost anything and it wouldn't have been something he'd heard before. And yet I could think of nothing to say. I was boring. That was why Jeff got tired of me.

Brian tapped the side of his coffee cup with his thumb. "My friends say that having a conversation with me is like talking to the school guidance counselor."

"Oh yeah?" I countered. "Well, my friends say. . ." I had to pause then because I couldn't remember what they'd say—it had been so long since I'd talked to any of my friends. My *real* friends. I remembered what *she* said, though. . . .

"What do your friends say?" Brian asked. His voice was low, almost hypnotic.

And I could still see her face. I don't think I'll ever

forget the defensive look she got on her face when I confronted her. "That he was going to leave me anyway," I said softly, still marveling at her nerve after all these years. "That it was not her fault." She had even cried, as if she were the one who had been hurt instead of me.

"What?"

I squeezed my eyes shut, trying to hold back the memories along with the tears, but while I could keep the water out of my eyes, the vision of Linda would not go away. "She said that if it hadn't been her, it would have been somebody else, and don't you see that it's better this way, better for the kids, to have him close by."

"Who said that?"

"My best friend, Linda." Hot tears poured down my cheeks as I forced myself to open my eyes. "Former best friend." That was the past. This was the present. The man I had here in the room with me now was the present. The vision I saw when I closed my eyes, that blond-haired betrayer, was in the past.

"Your best friend and your. . ."

"Husband, yes."

"That must have been horrifying."

"It—it was." But as I talked about it now, it didn't seem to hurt quite so much. I sniffed. "I need a tissue."

He stepped over to the counter, reached for the box, and handed me a tissue. "Do you want to tell me any more?"

It was funny, but now I did. I wanted Brian to feel that same sense of indignation that I had felt that day, and every day since. But I had to blow my nose first.

"Okay." I sniffed again as I tossed the tissue in the trash can. "I don't know whose fault it was."

"He was married," Brian said quickly. "The fault belonged to both."

"Yeah, you're right." I leaned back against the kitchen counter. "They were both to blame."

He nodded. "Absolutely."

"So anyway," I said with a sniff, "when I asked Jeff, he didn't even deny it." I felt my lip quiver a bit at the memory but kept going. "H–he said he was glad it was in the open now so he didn't have to sneak around anymore. He said I was. . ." I stopped, not wanting Brian to feel sorry for me. I cleared my throat. "He moved in with Linda. Two houses away. We could hear them from our backyard, talking, laughing, playing with her kids."

"That's pretty low."

"He should have sunk through the earth and come out on the other side," I agreed. "So anyway, the kids and I moved. Here." I waved toward the kitchen full of builder's grade appliances, the cheap vinyl flooring in the entry, the living/dining room painted in generic neutral colors. "It's not much, but it's all mine."

"And you don't want to let anyone else ruin it."

"Yeah, I guess so." I blew my nose again.

"Well, it's too late now." He smiled gently. "You've violated your rule. You've let me in."

I squinted at him. "I didn't think there was much danger that you'd have an affair with Jeff."

"The only danger is that you will let the despicable actions of two people ruin your life forever."

"I'm not." I started back over toward the table and

away from the box of tissues, because I was determined not to need them again. "I've started over."

"Have you?"

"Yes." I plopped back in my chair. "The kids are enrolled in great schools, Alicia is in lots of plays and takes classes at a studio, and we found a wonderful Cub Scout troop for Evan, and he plays spring and fall soccer and was invited to try out for the travel team next—"

He sat down across from me, staring me straight in the eye. "I don't mean the kids. Have you started *your* life over?"

"The kids *are* my life. And don't think that's just because of the divorce." I fiddled with the handle on my coffee mug. "It's because I know there's only a short time before they're grown and on their own. I want to make the most of my time with them."

There. I'd said it all. Now he knew everything about me, all the ugly, gory details. I had blown my nose so many times that it was probably bright red now. But I felt better anyway. Lighter somehow, as if I'd been wearing training weights on my ankles all day and had just now taken them off. As if I might float away at any moment.

I wanted him to spill his guts about something, too—to get the sense of relief and maybe feel embarrassed and grateful at the same time, as I did.

Maybe I should ask him about the woman on the brochure. His wife. The beautiful, talented woman he must miss very much. Maybe he would welcome the chance to talk about her.

I cleared my throat. "Since I'm running low on

tissues, we need to stop talking about me now. So how long have you volunteered at the 1776 House?"

He winced. "I really wish they would refer to it as the Barnswallow House, or even the Bird in Hand. There is no reason to attach the year 1776 to the site— it just gives people the idea that we had something to do with the war or the Declaration."

"I take it you've been there awhile?" His vehemence made me suddenly nervous. I so desperately wanted to cross him off that list of suspects, and he just kept reasserting the possibility of his own guilt.

"Chloe and I started there about ten years ago."

I offered an encouraging smile. "It must be hard some days to be there without her."

His face went blank for a moment. Then he turned toward the front door. "Did you say the kids would be home about now? I thought I heard a car."

I sighed. Either he was making this up to avoid my question or Jeff had pulled up in his new convertible to discharge two children who would find Mom's minivan very dull in comparison.

"I don't hear anything. But it is getting late." I offered him an easy exit after my awkward comment.

He pulled up the sleeve of his sweater to look at his watch. "Wow. Time flies when you're. . .you know."

"What? Being attacked by the dog? Wiping dessert off the floor?"

"Having fun," he insisted. His smile brought back a little of the sense of closeness we had shared earlier. I wished I'd asked about something other than the pretty woman at the spinning wheel.

Before I realized it, he was putting on his jacket.

"Thanks for inviting me over."

I smiled. "Thanks for coming." I concentrated hard to keep the smile genial and friendly while I opened the door for him.

"See you on Saturday?" He sounded hopeful.

"Oh yeah. Of course." *For a few more weeks.*

## 12

On Saturdays, I always tried to get from the house to the van without being seen in my petticoats and apron, but this time my neighbor caught me.

"Good morning, Karen!" Amy waved from her front yard where she was watering flowers.

Could I pretend I hadn't noticed her? No, that would be rude. "Mornin'!" I called back. I couldn't wave because I had a basket of shortbread and laundry in one arm and my keys, cell phone, and sunglasses in the other. As goofy as I felt dressed in colonial clothes, I felt even goofier in colonial clothes wearing sunglasses and driving a minivan.

Since the kids were at their dad's this weekend, I got ready earlier and arrived at the site an hour before it opened to the public, so it would be less chaotic for me than last Saturday had been. I fully expected Paula and Patty to press me for details about my dinner with Brian, and I wasn't ready to talk about it yet. I just needed some quiet time to look around by myself and think.

That was the plan, anyway. But when I walked into the gift shop, Ann Bleckenstrauss and Eileen McGregor were tearing through things in a manner that looked even more frantic than last week.

"Balloons missing again?" I joked.

"No." Mrs. McGregor stood stiffly, stepped away from the cabinet she had been examining, and focused a withering gaze on me. "We are missing the proceeds of the raffle."

"And the bake sale," Ann added without looking up from the box she was pawing through. "Over seven hundred dollars."

My stomach plummeted down to somewhere in the vicinity of my knees. "The money is missing?"

"Yes." Mrs. McGregor practically stared a hole through me, and I could well understand why. She had paid DS Investigations a substantial amount of money to recover stolen property, and so far all I had done was preside over another theft.

"Have you called the police?" This could mean the end of our involvement in the case. Mrs. McGregor might decide it wasn't worth it to pay investigators when the government would provide them for free.

"Not yet." Ann sighed and set down a set of salt and pepper shakers shaped like cherry trees. "We haven't established for certain that it was stolen. It may just be misplaced. I really hate to think that someone entrusted with the money might have actually absconded with it." She shook her head sadly.

I found it easier to look at Ann's sorrowful face than at Mrs. McGregor's angry one. "Who had it last?"

"We're not quite sure." Mrs. McGregor stepped back over to the cabinet but kept her stern gaze focused on me. "We know that you worked at the table most of the day, and Ann, of course."

"And John," I added. "The carpenter guy. He helped me."

"You know, I think I asked him to help me clean up," Ann said thoughtfully as she replaced a package of George Washington crazy straws back into their box. "You don't suppose he—"

Mrs. McGregor held up her hand to interrupt. "I don't *like* to suppose that any of our volunteers would deliberately do anything to harm the 1776 House. But we must accept the possibilities and act accordingly. We must find out whether *anyone else* had access to the money, particularly at the end of the day." She stared pointedly at me again, leaving no doubt as to her meaning. I had an additional assignment. And while Dave would be pleased with the extra hours and money this might involve, I felt as though I had already let our client down.

I nodded and started out toward the yard.

"Oh, and, Karen," Mrs. McGregor added in acid tones. "Don't forget that Lucinda Fotheringill and the delegation from the DAP will be here on October 17. We've waited six years for this visit, and we want everything to be perfect. If we have the right look, they're likely to feature us in their magazine. So we've had the kitchen walls whitewashed and new bed curtains made for the first bedchamber. We want things to stay clean and neat."

"I'll keep that in mind." She was reminding me of the deadline. I had only a little over two weeks to find the thief—and get the notes back.

The bake sale theft really threw me. Not only did it make me look incompetent, but it made John look much more likely as a suspect for everything. I felt like an idiot for not paying more attention to him right off the bat. Here I worked with the guy for a large part of the afternoon and really learned very little.

So now I needed to shadow him more than ever. But I didn't want him to realize that's what I was doing.

He was out in the yard working with a tool that shaved off little curls each time he passed it across the surface of the wood. I offered to set up another laundry demonstration in the yard so that I would be close to him throughout the day. It also gave me an excuse to ask Brian for his shirt, but I didn't think I actually would.

While I was wringing out towels for about the forty-seventh time and wishing I could think up a less strenuous excuse to stay out in the yard, I saw Mrs. McGregor stalk out of the house and over to John's display. They spoke for several minutes, her head bobbing up and down like a chicken intent on picking up every scrap within reach. He continued to work, which gave him a ready reason not to look her in the eye. She eventually sailed back into the house, petticoats and apron strings trailing in her wake.

A few minutes later, Paula also set out from the house with a big bundle wrapped in her apron. She stopped in front of me and looked behind her as if she were a bank robber absconding with a bag of stolen loot. "What have you got in the pot now?" She nodded toward the big iron kettle boiling on a tripod over a fire.

I looked at the towels I had wrung out, which were really old cotton diapers that I had used as spit-up cloths when Evan was a baby. "Three diapers."

"Then there's room for this." She unfolded her apron to reveal heavy red, white, and blue fabric, which she cast into the pot. She took up a three-pronged stick called a "washing molly" and stirred the fabric with an almost evil grin of satisfaction.

"We don't usually boil colored clothes, do we?" I noticed that the water had already turned pink. "Doesn't it fade them?"

"Yes." Her grin widened.

"And that's okay?"

"We need to fade these curtains. They're far too bright—look like they just came off the bolt."

I peered into the pot, where the water was now almost magenta. Not only would the curtains surely fade, but the diapers would turn pink. It was a good thing Evan was long finished with them.

"Those are the new bed curtains, aren't they?" I asked.

"One of them. They're too big to boil all at once." She glanced toward the house again. "And less likely to be noticed if they're only missing one at a time."

"Are you afraid the house ladies won't approve?"

"I'm not *afraid* of any of them. But I know they won't approve, and we don't have time for debate here. We've got to get the site ready for the DAP photographer."

So she was determined and saw sneaky behavior as legitimate means to her end. Perhaps she and John might have worked together on the theft—he to profit and she to rid the site of the detested notes.

As if she could read my mind, she peered behind me to where John was working with that wood-shaving tool. "You've heard about the money from last week, haven't you?" she asked in a low voice. "We all know who took it. He's got some nerve to just stand there, acting so innocent. I asked him about it as he walked in this morning, and he pretended to be all shocked and outraged." She shook her head disparagingly. "I don't know why we tolerate him here. He should be asked to leave. Then you'd see—all these thefts would miraculously cease."

" 'All these thefts'? There have been others?"

"Well, Eileen seems to think those so-called Washington notes were stolen. And while I know they're worthless, there are other people"—she stared pointedly at John—"who could fool some collector into believing they are genuine."

I lowered my voice. "Why are you so certain he's the thief?"

"He's been caught stealing before. At one of the sutler's booths at the Fort Frederick Market Fair last spring."

"Sutler's booths?"

"A sutler is a merchant, usually one who sells in military encampments, and Fort Frederick is mostly civilian, so—"

I needed to steer her back on topic. "Was he caught stealing at one of the booths?"

"Not exactly. While he was there, Brian recognized an elaborate weather vane that one of the sutlers was selling. It was one Brian had made the year before for a buyer who never showed up to claim it. He was going to offer it for sale in the gift shop, but it mysteriously vanished. Just like the raffle money. Anyway, he recognized the vane, and the sutler said he had taken it in exchange for a powder horn with carvings of a map of the county on it. Brian had seen John with a powder horn just like that. The sutler said the horn he'd traded John was worth at least four hundred dollars. *Four hundred dollars.* That's money that should have gone to the site. Instead, John kept it for himself. Lousy thief."

So now I understood the warning that Patty had given Brian on my first visit. *"Don't take anything in trade. You don't want to end up holding stolen merchandise."* But Brian hadn't seemed too worried. In fact, he had even made something for John. Obviously he didn't hold a grudge against him. Why? Had the two of them secretly worked out a deal to defraud the site? Had they worked together to remove the Washington notes?

This situation was giving me a headache. I didn't want Brian implicated in any way in all this.

"You plainly need some respite!" Paula said in a loud voice for the benefit of the group of Girl Guides that had just stepped out of the house. "You need to keep your wits about you, or a thief might make light with your laundry." Her gaze strayed to John for a moment as he set down his tools and started toward the kitchen.

"Huh?" I blinked. "Do you seriously think someone's going to steal the diapers?" I whispered to her.

"Clothing is valuable," she answered in a much louder voice. "Even old rags can be sold. If you don't keep watch over your lines, the clothing might disappear, and you'd have to answer for it."

"Well, good," I muttered to myself as I sat down on a stump, wishing for some hand lotion. "Instead of watching the grass grow, I get to watch the laundry dry."

"Take yourself to the kitchen to see if the cook can

find you a few scraps. I shall watch your wash for you until you return," Paula ordered imperiously.

As I heaved myself to my feet and started toward the kitchen, she stepped over and whispered, "Patty's dying to know how dinner with Brian went, so don't disappoint her." She winked. Then she stalked over to the Girl Guides and started accusing them of trying to steal the stockings and diapers that sagged on the line because I hadn't wrung them out well enough.

The first thing I would do when I got home was kiss the washing machine. I could write poetry about the man who invented it.

Actually, it was probably a woman.

When I stepped into the kitchen, John was resting on a bench, drinking something out of a large tankard and eating a pork pasty. Patty stood by the fire, rubbing her eyes.

"Smoke?" I asked sympathetically. No matter which way I moved around a fire, the smoke always seemed to follow me.

"No," she answered with a sniff. "My eyes've been bothering me all morning. Allergies, I guess." She dabbed at one red-rimmed eye with the corner of her handkerchief. "I should carry antihistamines with me wherever I go this time of year."

I grinned. "They didn't have antihistamines in colonial days."

She pressed the handkerchief over her eyes. "Yes, and most of them died of smallpox or yellow fever before they could get old enough to worry about saggy eyelids. But I do, and I hate to keep rubbing my eyes like this."

"Maybe you should run to the drugstore."

"I would, but there's that group of visitors out there. They'll be coming in any minute, and I don't want them to miss the kitchen demonstration."

"I'll do it." I wanted to put my hand over my mouth, but it was too late.

"Do you think you can manage it for a few minutes?" Patty looked so hopeful that I hated to disappoint her with the truth.

"Yes," I lied. "Piece of cake."

She immediately started for the door, giving directions over her shoulder. "There *is* a cake, in fact, in there that you will need to add fresh coals to in a few minutes and will probably be done in a quarter of an hour. Keep the chicken spinning, of course. And keep the fire up so we'll have enough coals, and keep the cabbage pudding at a slow boil." She paused and pointed to the black pots by the fire as she completed her mental tally. "The only thing you need to do to the pumpkin soup is to stir it to keep it from burning. I'll be back in a jiff." She scooted out the door before I could ask which covered black kettle held which of the aforementioned dishes.

I tried to figure out just how long it would take for her to walk to her car, drive to the store, select her medicine, stand in line—

"You need to add more wood." John nodded toward the fire, where the merry crackling flames had sunk into sullen red coals.

I picked up the nearest fireplace implement and waved it toward the coals. "These are what I need to put on the cake pan, though, right?"

"Yes, but you need to keep burning wood to create

a steady supply of coals." John stood, walked to the wood bin, and selected two split chunks of wood. He laid them carefully on the coals.

I waited in vain for them to burst into flame. "Why aren't they burning?"

"They will." He looked at me with a skeptical frown. "You don't know much, do you? S'pose I'll have to take over fire duty. You just mind the food so we'll have somethin' to eat. "

"Thanks." I smiled. I was grateful for the help, if not the grudging manner in which it was offered.

"But," he warned, "I'll do it only if you refrain from mentioning anything about the raffle and bake sale, because I'm sick of hearing about it."

Here was my chance to get him on my side. "Me, too. Everyone keeps asking me questions. I'm beginning to wonder if people think *I* took the money, since I spent so much time working at the table."

He just looked at me for a moment. "No," he said at last. "Everyone suspects me."

"I guess it could have been any of us. We could all be suspects."

"No." He shook his head. "Everyone thinks I took it because of a mistake I made last year. Now anytime something is missing, they automatically assume I took it. They don't even bother looking. If Patty set down her spoon and couldn't find it, she'd probably send Paula to accuse me of stealing it."

"It's that bad?"

"How about those note artifacts that are missing? I don't think anyone's even looked for them. Someone probably took them out to polish the case or something and misplaced them. I'll bet no one's even looked. They just think I took them." He pointed toward the house. "I saw Paula coming out of that room at the very end of the day they went missing, but did they even consider the possibility that she might have taken the things?" He shook his head again. "No. They all think it must have been me."

"What's burning?" A girl walked into the kitchen holding her nose.

"Is that all you kids can ever say?" I grumbled as I stepped over to the fire. I wanted to question John, not display my lack of knowledge about cooking to a bunch of overly critical Girl Guides. I hoped I had time for one more question before the rest of them descended on us. "It's not unusual for Paula to be up in that part of the house at closing time, is it?"

John scratched his head. "Well, maybe not. But actually, I don't think it was Paula. I think it was Patty."

"Patty?"

He waved as if it made no difference. "Or Paula. Whoever it was had changed back into regular clothes. It was one of them. But they're never suspected of anything, oh no." John shook his head. "I'm going out to split some more wood for you."

"Thanks." I smiled, hoping he would return soon so I could find out more about what Paula had been doing near the bedchamber on the day of the theft. I tried to picture the layout of the upstairs of the house, wondering where John had been when he saw her.

"Okay, girls." The perky redheaded leader clapped her hands as she stepped into the kitchen. "Everybody step all the way in so you can see the cooking demonstration." She turned to me with a simpering smile. "What are you making for us today, goodwife?"

"Charcoal, probably," I muttered as I lifted the lid on the first kettle. "This is a cake." Since I hadn't added more coals to the lid, it hadn't burned. Yet. "I have to add more coals to keep it hot." I tried to tilt the layer of gray ashes off into the corner, but instead I flipped the lid completely off; it hit the fire and sent a spray of ashes out over everything in the vicinity, including my petticoat, the shoes of the girls nearest to me, and the top of the cake in the open kettle. "And that's why they call it ashcake," I announced for the edification of the girls.

"I thought ashcakes were wrapped in corn husks and baked directly in the ashes," the scout leader objected with a frown.

"There were many different regional variations. Now, over here we have. . ." I let my words trail off as I lifted the lid on the next mystery kettle. "Pumpkin soup." I stirred it, or at least the top of it. Some of it on the bottom seemed stuck to the pan, and I thought it should probably just stay that way. "And in this pot here"—I swung out the crane to see the water that was supposed to be boiling was barely warm—"is a cabbage pudding."

"Eww." Several girls grimaced.

One of them shook her head. "And I thought rice pudding was icky."

I found their "grossed out" reaction oddly satisfying, especially since I had tried the dish in question, a sort of meat loaf wrapped in cabbage leaves, and knew it to be pretty good.

"Is that a real chicken on that string there?" Another girl pointed toward the side of the fireplace.

"Oh yes." I smiled. "All the food we use here is real."

"Why is it on a string? And why is it black?" she asked.

"Black?" I peered to the side of the fireplace, and there, just as she'd pointed out, was a black chicken hanging on a string. I was supposed to keep winding up the string so it would turn and cook on all sides. Obviously I hadn't fulfilled that duty, either. "Blackened chicken was very popular in this part of Maryland," I announced. "Only pepper was too expensive, so they just blackened it by leaving it in the fire."

"You're messing with their impressionable little minds," John whispered as he added more wood to the fire. "I like it!"

At first I grinned. But then I started to feel bad. Although it was fun to make up answers, I really wasn't furthering the goals of the site. I remembered Brian's gentle lessons and Patty's detailed demonstrations and decided that while making up lies might provide a quick answer, it was a lousy idea.

I turned back to the girls. "Do you really think that's why there's a black chicken hiding back there?"

Most of the girls shook their heads.

"Really, I was supposed to keep winding up the string like this." I picked up a pot holder, took hold of the skewer at the bottom of the bird, and twisted it numerous times. "And then it would unwind and turn the chicken like a rotisserie. But I forgot, and so it burned on the side that was left by the fire."

"That's because you have too much to mind," Patty announced.

I hadn't seen her come in. I considered scrunching down low and trying to sneak out with the Girl Guide troop before she could blame me for ruining all her food.

But instead of reproaching me, she chided the young visitors. "Turning the chicken is a job for one of you children!" Patty eyed them all in turn. "Well, don't just stand there lollygagging. Get to work."

The girls all took three steps back.

"I'll help you," I offered. "Anyone want to try it?"

One of the girls finally raised her hand. As I showed her how to wind up the string without touching the hot skewer, I wished Brian would come in. But just as he missed my earlier moment of infamy, he also missed my reparations. Patty, however, smiled.

And she didn't complain about the destruction of her food, either. The pumpkin soup that wasn't stuck to the bottom of the pot was delicious, and the chicken was only burned on one side. We set these out for lunch for the volunteers, along with a loaf of bread Patty had brought from home. John, Paula, and Ann all stopped by to eat, but though I kept watching for him at the door, Brian never appeared.

I was starting to wonder whether he was avoiding me.

## 13

We ate. I took out the cake, an ugly brown lump that smelled of butter and nutmeg, and set it on the windowsill to cool.

Then we started to clean up.

"Now that I have you to help me, I'll have more time to make bread here." Patty smiled at me as she removed the loaf from the table and stashed it in a covered basket.

I cringed. "Well, I might not be able to come *every* week. The kids' schedules will be getting pretty busy soon."

Patty sighed. "It's terrible just how busy everyone gets. All the running from place to place. I think that's why the 'good old days' seem so appealing. There was no less work, but a lot less commuting." She wiped the crumbs off the table into her apron, stepped to the doorway, and shook the crumbs out into the grass. Then she whirled around to face me with sudden intensity. "Since he isn't here, I'll ask you now." She stepped closer and looked up at me with a smile that was suddenly shy. "How did your date with Brian go?"

"We just had dinner. It wasn't a date." I looked at the doorway before I could stop myself.

"It wasn't?" Patty frowned. "Well, it should have been. We told you, Brian needs to go on a few dates. He's not ready to marry again, but Chloe's been gone for almost six years, and he needs to start rebuilding his life."

"What, um, happened to Chloe?"

"Cancer. Turns out that was why they were never able to have kids, poor thing. But she never complained. The woman was the closest thing to a saint I ever saw."

"That's probably why Brian doesn't want to date anyone else," I said slowly.

"That's just why he *should*. The longer he waits, the more difficult it will get. And look at him—he's so good with kids. Wouldn't he make the perfect dad?"

"Yeah," I agreed, "he would." But of course I had not been thinking of that at all. I just thought he made a great guy to spend time with, except that he sort of made it hard to breathe at times.

Like now, for instance. I wondered whether thoughts of Brian had made me breathless and light-headed, because what I was seeing made no sense. Patty had taken a candle, lit it from the fire, and was now holding it up to the whitewashed wall near the fireplace.

"Are you trying to start the building on fire?" I asked finally.

She laughed. "It would take a long time this way. Plaster doesn't burn. That's why it was used to cover walls whenever people could afford it."

"Then what are you—"

"Smoke stains. The kitchen fire is going all the time. The walls should be stained from the smoke."

I stared at the white expanse of wall on each side of the fireplace. "Won't they get stained from your cooking fire?"

"Yes, over time they will. But we don't have much time."

"You don't?"

"The DAP photographer will be here in a couple of weeks. We want the site to look authentic and worn."

I stared at her for a moment. "Wait. Didn't Mrs. McGregor just have these walls painted?"

Patty grimaced. "She did. Without even asking the Property Committee." Having achieved the proper blackness with her candle, she moved to another spot on the wall.

"So—I don't understand." I now had a reason to ask some questions. "Who makes the decisions about these kinds of things? Who decides how the walls should look, and the displays, and so on?"

"Well. . ." Paula held her candle to the wall. "The Property Committee is supposed to make decisions about the grounds, and that includes the outbuildings like this one."

"What about the displays in the house?"

"There's another committee. The House Committee."

"So they decide about things like the new bed curtains that Paula decided needed to be faded."

Patty turned to face me with a grin. "Yes."

"Is Paula on the House Committee? Because if so, I can't imagine she would have agreed to display the Washington notes that she thought were fake."

Patty turned back to the wall. "Paula *was* on the House Committee, but she got disgusted and quit because she was always outvoted by Ann and Eileen and their friends."

"So she probably voted against displaying the notes?"

"She got up a petition to have the notes taken out."

"Is that why they're gone now?"

Patty looked at me for a moment. "No. She didn't get enough of the members' signatures to bring the petition to the board."

I stepped closer to her. "So if Paula didn't get the notes taken out, what happened to them?"

"I don't know," Patty said quickly, looking intently at the candle in front of her. "Paula doesn't know, either."

*Aha! Patty is covering for Paula.* "Well," I prodded, "they couldn't have just vanished. Though I guess you probably wanted them to."

"Oh no." She turned to me with a look of almost horror on her face. "I'd hate to have any artifact disappear. Something of value can be learned from each of them."

"Even a fake?"

She shook her head. "We don't know for certain that the notes are fake."

"I thought you did tests or checked records or something."

"We did check records, and that makes the story of the notes implausible. But not impossible." Patty waved her candle for emphasis. "And who knows—the notes may have been written by someone else almost as important. What if they were written by a Civil War general instead of a Revolutionary one? What if they were written by a prankster trying to cash in on Washington's popularity just after his death? They would still be valuable and worthy of display."

I grinned. "So you don't hate them?"

"Not at all."

"Paula does, I think." I watched to gauge her reaction.

Patty's aura of certainty dissolved. She looked down for a moment before turning back to the wall. "She does."

And I had to ask, even if I didn't want to know the answer. "Brian didn't like the notes either, did he?"

She shook her head. A weight settled in the bottom of my stomach.

"Did he think they might have some value, like you do?"

"I don't know. We never really discussed it." Though she was partially turned away from me, I could see her frown. *Is she covering for Brian, too?*

I decided I had learned all I wanted to know for the present. Patty now had her mouth clamped shut and probably wouldn't talk to me again for the rest of the day. I should go back to the laundry setup and start questioning Paula. Or, as much as I hated to admit it, Brian.

But I did not want to leave Patty with this sense of coldness between us. "Can I help you with the smoke stains?" I asked softly.

Her face immediately brightened. "You can. We have to work fast, before another group of visitors comes by."

I nodded. "This would look pretty odd."

"Indeed it would. I think we might get more smoke from a fat lamp than a modern candle, so maybe I'll have you try that."

"What's a fat lamp?"

Patty grunted as she reached down into a basket under the worktable. "It's like an oil lamp, but you can use different types of fat. I've been experimenting with bacon grease." She held up a black iron implement about the size of a large Christmas ornament. It basically looked like a bowl on a hook. "Have you ever heard of a betty lamp?"

"Is that what that is?"

"No, this is a much more basic design, not much different from lamps made thousands of years ago, though those would have been made of clay. Betty lamps are a little more refined than this." When she waved the lamp toward me, I could see something yellow stuck to the bottom.

"I think there's something on it. Looks like a piece of paper." I reached for it and pulled off a small Post-it note, half soaked through with grease. "It just says 'Athena.' Do you need to keep it?"

"No." A strange look flashed across her face, and I wondered if the name upset her for some reason, but then she sneezed, so I assumed the strange look was simply a pre-sneeze grimace. She smiled. "Athena is my cat. That note is to remind me to take her to the vet."

I started to put the paper in the trash bag, which was hidden in a cask in the corner.

She waved toward the fireplace. "You can just put that right in the fire. We try to burn up as much of our trash as possible."

I was already closer to the trash can than to the fire, but she seemed very insistent, still waving me toward the fireplace. So I stepped back over and tossed the note into the fire. She watched as the paper turned black and crumbled to ash. Only then did she turn her attention back to the lamp.

"I hope she's not sick," I said.

Patty blinked. "Who?"

"Your cat."

"Oh no. Just shots. So what do you think of the lamp? I really think we should be using more lamps and fewer candles here."

Patty went on to describe how candles were made from various substances, and I tried to pay attention because I knew this was the sort of thing Brian thought I was interested in. So I tried to be. But instead I wondered about that piece of paper. There was no real reason to wonder about it. I left Post-it notes on things all over the office. And Patty probably just wanted the note burned because it was greasy. But there had been a look of satisfaction on her face that seemed to transcend mere gratification with the trash disposal process. Before I could give any more thought to her reaction, however, Paula came in with none-too-gentle hints about the need to return to my laundry demonstration. So it was time to move from one sister to the other.

I followed Paula out to the yard and tried to think up some casual questions to lead up to the real topics of interest. But before I could ask about Athena or the notes or anything else, Paula flung a wad of heavy wet fabric into my arms.

"Help me wring this out." She took one end and twisted it while I twisted the other.

Okay, so we wouldn't talk about anything that would help me determine whether Patty was covering for her sister. We would talk about bed curtains. "Did it fade like you had hoped?" I asked.

"No." Her voice was sullen, her expression even more so. Frown lines etched in her forehead made her look much older than her sister.

I tried to find something hopeful to say. "It does look a little duller, at least."

"I guess." She twisted even harder. When she was satisfied that we had wrung as much water from the curtain as was humanly possible, she gathered it up and stalked back toward the house.

And I went back to washing dish-towels-that-were-really-diapers, having gained nothing except an even deeper appreciation of the washing machine.

Secretly I was rather pleased that Paula's plan to fade the curtains had not worked. What right did she have to destroy everyone else's hard work? Popping balloons, ruining new curtains—all because she was certain she knew best. And I had this gut feeling she was to blame for the missing notes, too, though I wasn't sure yet how she had done it. Had she left the display case open and tempted John to take them? Had she left the case open and tempted a dog to eat them? Had she and Brian simply moved the notes to the attic to get them out of the public's eye?

I didn't like that last option as much, but it presented itself nevertheless. Besides, if Brian was avoiding me, why should I want to protect him? He pried open my most embarrassing secrets and then left me flat.

"Hi, Karen." His voice was so soft I could barely hear it.

I looked up from the pink diapers I was wringing out.

He wasn't standing quite as straight as he usually did, and the tilt of his head, the shy smile, all made him look quite bashful. And his voice grew even softer. "I wanted to thank you for inviting me over the other night."

"What?" It took a few moments for the words to sink in, but I could see immediately that he was embarrassed, now growing red in the face even as I watched. Was he embarrassed because everyone thought we went on a date? Was he trying to find a polite way to tell me it had been a mistake?

"It was nothing," I said gruffly. *Okay, you've been polite. Now you can leave.*

"I, um, was wondering if you, um. . ."

This man, who played with molten metal for fun and willingly struck up conversations with middle-schoolers, the man who always spoke with quiet authority, was now just unintelligibly quiet.

"I didn't quite get that," I admitted.

He dug the toe of his buckled shoe into the grass, just as Evan might have done before confessing that no, he had not remembered to take out the trash again this week. "I hoped you might let me return the favor," he said at last. "Let me take you to dinner."

"Oh." So this wasn't the awkward good-bye. It was a request for a second date. I decided I should probably stand up, because I didn't look very romantic bent over a washtub. As I stood, I stepped on the hem of my skirt, staggered forward, and grabbed at a laundry line for support. A wet diaper slapped against my face.

I peeled the wet fabric off my cheek. "I would love to go to dinner with you." I guess I felt I had to answer as quickly as possible before he retracted the offer.

He reached out his hand to steady me as I disentangled myself from the laundry line. "Are you okay?"

"Oh yeah, of course." I tried to smile, but I had just stepped into the washtub, and the cold rinse water was quite a shock. Even the warm sensation of his hand on my arm was not quite enough to prevent me from grimacing.

"Not getting cold feet, are you?" He grinned.

"Just one." I pulled my foot out of the tub, took off the wet shoe, and emptied out the water. A surprisingly small amount came out. "These things really soak up water, don't they?"

He nodded. "That shoe's going to be wet for a while. Why don't you sit down and rest, and I'll see if I can find you another pair." He steered me over to a tree stump.

"What's the matter?" Patty immediately rushed out of the kitchen as if she'd been watching us the whole time. "Did you hurt yourself?"

"Not at all. I just needed a footbath. Only I forgot to take off my shoes first. Brian's going to look for a dry pair for me."

"Oh no, he isn't," she said with a stern glance at him. "Paula and I reorganized the women's clothing closet, and I'm not going to have him mess it up. I'll look for shoes for you. And, Brian, stay here with her to make sure she gives that foot a rest."

"But I didn't hurt my foot." I stood up to demonstrate.

She pushed me back down. "You can never be too careful." And then she winked as she turned away toward the house.

Brian looked at me. Then he looked at the grass. Then he looked at me. Then he addressed a question to my foot. "So, uh, do you like ethnic food?"

We were back on the subject of dinner, apparently, just as Patty would have wanted. "Yes." I nodded. "Anything but sushi."

He stared at my foot for a moment and then at the washtub. We both watched pink diapers flap in the breeze for what seemed like an inordinate length of time. Then finally he looked me in the eye. "There's a special event I'd like to take you to." He took a deep breath. "Next Saturday night at six?"

I nodded again. "Sure." I was about to smile, not really believing this was happening, when an unpleasant reminder tugged at the back of my mind. "Oh, I can't next Saturday. Can we make it the weekend after?"

"You can't?" He let out a big breath of air. "Why not?"

"I have the kids next weekend." Plans of my own could wait until the weekends when they were with their father. Especially dates. Who knew what they would think about me going on a date?

"Oh, okay." His face fell, but he recovered quickly. "Some other time, then."

I had hoped he would take my earlier suggestion that we make a date for the following Saturday, but he didn't.

Though I thought about repeating the suggestion, just to test his reaction, I decided to wait and check with the kids first to see how they felt.

We both sat in awkward silence for a while after that. I tried to think about questions I should ask John, or how to get Paula to admit she had been in the first bedchamber at the time the notes disappeared. I tried to think of the schedule for the upcoming week, whether we had a full pack meeting at Cub Scouts and whether Alicia's next audition was this Thursday or next. But my mind kept straying, and instead I would think about the way the breeze ruffled through Brian's hair and how much I wanted to touch it. I had never known a guy with long hair—did it feel different from a woman's hair? Was it coarse?

He noticed I was staring and looked away.

Patty was taking an incredibly long time with the shoes.

"You know, I'm really not hurt, and you don't need to wait out here with me." I put on a smile. "I'm old enough to be by myself."

"Yeah, I guess I'd better be getting back to the forge." He stood and looked around the yard as if hoping a big group would enter the blacksmith shop so he had an excuse to leave me. But the only people besides us in the yard were two little girls chasing butterflies by the springhouse. Their mother would occasionally stick her head out of the gift shop to ascertain their whereabouts.

Why was no one else in the yard? Where was John? "Did John leave?" I called to Brian as he walked away.

"I think so. He mentioned something about being sick."

He hadn't seemed sick at all in the kitchen. But he

did say he was sick of being asked about the missing raffle money.

And that was a shame, because eventually I'd have to ask him about it, too. He was the only logical suspect for that theft.

Dave always said he had to be logical even if his suspects sometimes were not. And the remark about the best actors never setting foot on a stage. He said that, too.

Which made me think that I needed to find either a new field of work or at least a case in which none of the suspects were attractive, considerate, muscular, or even vaguely nice.

## 14

The look of disappointment on Brian's face when I rejected his dinner invitation haunted me for the rest of the afternoon and evening. It didn't haunt me in the sense that it scared me or even that it made me feel sad for him. It made me feel sad for myself. Like I was missing an opportunity.

But I reminded myself that I had plenty of time for me later. What mattered most was making time for my kids, because they wouldn't be around much longer. They were the important ones right now.

I ruffled Evan's hair, which was standing up in even more places than usual, as he came down for breakfast Monday morning. "So how about if we go bowling on Saturday while Alicia is at Carla's birthday party?"

"I don't think I'll have time, Mom. I'm sleeping over at Jeremy's, remember?"

"Sleeping over?"

"Yeah, remember? He asked me last week, but you said you couldn't say anything because it wasn't your weekend, so his mom invited me next Saturday instead." He grinned. "Only that's this Saturday now."

Vague recollections of that conversation filtered through my Monday morning mind. It had seemed so far away when we had talked about it. But it was indeed coming up this Saturday. Evan had a 3:00 soccer game and was supposed to go home from there with Jeremy. I wouldn't see him again until Sunday, probably midday. But that would give me extra time alone with Alicia. We could have dinner together before her friend Carla's roller dance party. And then make pancakes together Sunday morning.

I set microwaved pancakes on the table with fewer misgivings than usual. Though I didn't have time for a real breakfast on workdays, I would make up for it on Sunday with my girl. We would cook four different types of pancakes in all different shapes.

"Alicia?"

She flipped her hair out of her face just enough so that I could see one eye.

I tried to set the bottle of syrup on the table, but it was sticky. So when I lifted my hand, the bottle came back up with it. When I shook it loose, it skittered across the table and spun to a stop just inches shy of her orange juice glass. "Where would you like to go to dinner on Saturday? Evan has a sleepover, so it will be just us girls."

"Well, actually, Mom. . ." Alicia flipped her hair back into her face as if she didn't want to look at me. "Carla was going to ask her sister if she would take us to McDonald's before the party. It would be so cool to go with a high schooler. So if she says yes, can I go?"

When I didn't answer right away, she tucked a big wad of hair behind her ear, probably so she could see whether I was nodding yes. And eventually I did. But I felt a little like a deflated balloon—all buoyant with expectation one minute and simply flat the next. Alicia didn't want to be with me. And neither did Evan. Here I'd set aside precious time to spend with them, and they were too busy.

This was as it should be, I reminded myself as I ran

the syrup bottle under hot water to melt off the sticky goo on the outside. Parents groom their children to live their own lives. My little birds were taking practice flights in preparation to leave the nest for good one day.

That sounded like a line from a really bad song.

Alicia put the pancakes somewhere—I'm not sure she actually had time to put them in her mouth, but they were gone—and rose to leave. "Bye, Mom."

"Did you make your bed?"

She groaned. "It's just going to get messed up again tonight. Why do I have to make it?"

"Because I'm grooming you to live your own life." I left out the part about the bird leaving the nest, because it was simply too nauseating for this hour of the morning.

"Can you groom her to live my life, too?" Evan asked with a grin. "Since she's already gonna be upstairs?"

I smiled, my mood lifting already. "No, you have to live your own. I've already lived it for you too many times."

He tried to punch me on the arm, but I quickly smothered him with a hair-ruffling hug. And then I kissed him, noticing that his hair smelled a little sour, not sweet like when he was a young child and I washed it carefully for him each night.

When I said I'd lived his life too many times, I meant that I'd been having to make his bed for him most of the time lately. He understood that.

But now I realized I actually meant much more. I was still trying to live his life. And Alicia's. Because I no longer had one of my own.

Evan pulled away, shuffled off to the family room, and picked up the TV remote to watch cartoons until it was time to catch the bus. Alicia dashed down the stairs a moment later, picked up her book bag, and disappeared out the front door in a blur. I think she called "Bye" somewhere along the route, but it was frankly a little hard to tell.

———

Dave's voice rang out to greet me even before I had fully set foot inside the door to the office. "You need to call Mrs. McGregor!" he hollered in a thick, powdered-donut voice.

"Good morning to you, too!" I called back as I hung my jacket on the nearest antler.

"She left three messages on the answering machine about the money that's missing from a cake table or something. And she's called my cell phone twice since eight."

By this time I had reached his door. I leaned into his office. "And did you answer?"

"It's your case."

"Well, you know. . ." I stepped over to his desk to see what he was eating. "We did promise her that you would be working on the case, too. I think you need to put in at least a token appearance soon."

"When are they open?"

I peered into a half-empty box of mini donuts. "Most of them are there on Saturdays." I selected a plain brown donut, since all the coconut and powdered sugar donuts were gone.

"Most of who?"

"The suspects." The plain brown donut tasted about as exciting as it looked. I picked out one of the ones with the waxy chocolate coating. "Why don't you buy us real donuts once in a while?"

"Why don't you?"

"I buy the coffee."

"Okay, look. You tell Mrs. McGregor I'll come talk to her on Saturday. That should get her off my back for the rest of the week."

I debated whether to tell him that he would have to wear knee breeches and a puffy pirate shirt to fit in. I decided to make coffee instead.

"Hey, Karen," Dave called after me as I headed for the former closet that we'd turned into a kitchen area. "How's the case going, anyway?"

"Okay, I guess." I didn't know what to say. I sure hoped he hadn't expected me to have it closed by now. "I'll get a report to you this afternoon."

"I don't need a report," he hollered back. "Just tell me what's going on."

"But we need a weekly report for the file."

"We need a report for the file when the case is done. Just tell me what's happening. Get your coffee first. And bring me some. "

"I'll have to put yours in a paper cup, because your coffee mug isn't in here," I called back. I once made the mistake of looking through his office for his coffee cup and found it covered with so many different shades of growth that I wasn't sure if I should sterilize it or submit it to Scientific America with a grant proposal.

With fresh coffee in both hands, I headed into his office. Before I could sit down, I had to move a stack of folders from the chair onto the heater, so if the blower came on too strong, I ran the risk of being buried by a storm of flying papers. But then, everyone knows investigation work carries some inherent risks.

"Now, who are the suspects again?" Dave wiped powdered sugar off his lip and onto his sleeve.

"Paula Lowell is still the prime suspect. And John Holbrock is probably a close second. Patty Lowell, Brian Kieffer, and Ann Bleckenstrauss haven't been ruled out yet, either. And there was this dog. . . ." I was starting to get embarrassed about that theory after voicing it aloud.

"A dog?"

"Well, the missing artifact was made of leather," I said defensively.

"You're right not to discount any possibility," he admitted. "Where was the artifact when it was stolen?"

"In a locked case."

He took a big slurp of coffee. "Does the dog have unusually developed fine motor skills?"

"Well, I thought someone might have opened the case for him and let him do the rest."

"Why? Of what value are the stolen goods inside a dog's stomach?"

"Most of the suspects don't believe the stolen artifact has any value."

His face twisted into a lopsided quizzical expression. "They don't?"

I nodded. "They think it's a fake and just wanted it off display."

He pursed his lips for a moment. "And they would destroy the Washington whatever-they-weres to get them out of sight?"

"Yeah. Well, at least some of them probably would." Paula would, without a doubt. But John would most likely want to sell or trade them, and Ann would trade them to incur favor with the DAP. Patty might not destroy the notes either, since she said she thought there was a chance the notes might be of some value if they were analyzed. And Brian? I still was avoiding considering him a real suspect.

"I don't think it was the dog," I said at last.

Dave nodded. "Well, he didn't work alone, in any case. Who had keys?"

"Mrs. McGregor and Ann. Paula, Patty, and Brian had some keys, but not the keys to the case in question."

"You don't consider Ann, Patty, and Brian likely suspects, I take it."

"N–no."

"Are you certain?"

"Oh, I suppose anyone could be a suspect, even Mrs. McGregor. Maybe she's paying us to deflect blame from herself."

"If she is, I'm willing to let her. Are you certain about the others?"

In all honesty, I was not certain about anything. I shook my head. "No."

Dave slurped his coffee again. "Then why don't you consider them *likely* suspects?"

I fought back a wave of nervous tension. I did have reasons for my suspicions, or lack thereof. Dave was not doubting me, necessarily; he just wanted to know my reasoning. I started to tick off the suspects on my fingers. "One. Ann doesn't seem like the type to sneak or steal to get what she wants. She was appalled at the idea that someone might have embezzled the bake sale money. Two. Patty seemed to think the notes might have some value, so I don't think she'd try to remove them. And three. . ."

"This Brian fellow?"

"Yeah." My logic failed here. I had no real reason not to consider him a suspect. My own personal feelings had interfered with my ability to investigate. I shrugged miserably. "I guess I trust him."

Dave leaned forward with a menacing, protective-brother look in his eye. "Don't trust *anyone* until the case is closed. Suspects will try any number of tricks to get in your good graces. This guy might flatter you, offer help, even ask you out."

"I am undercover," I said lamely, not even convincing myself. "He doesn't know I'm investigating him."

"I wouldn't bet on it." He leaned back in his chair. "You've been at this now for what, two weeks?"

"Just over three." Had Brian known the whole time? Was he only pretending to like me? Had I missed important evidence because I was more interested in dating than in making the case?

"All of 'em might be onto you." Dave turned to his calendar. "You're right—I do need to get out there and find out for sure. You said most of 'em won't be there 'til Saturday?"

"Yes." I nodded miserably.

He nodded. "All right. I'll be there when they open."

The phone rang, and I used that as an excuse to run to my desk, grateful that I could hold the tears in check long enough so that he wouldn't see. "G—good morning," I blubbered into the receiver. Dave didn't trust me, didn't think I knew what I was doing.

And he was right.

"Don't hang up!" a cheerful voice ordered. "I have exciting news about timeshares."

I hung up.

I didn't know what I was doing. Maybe everybody at the site knew I was an investigator and they were all creating stories behind my back. And Brian had asked me out to flatter me, get on my good side. He had even managed to trick me into asking him out first.

I had until Saturday to prove to Dave that I was doing something right.

———

As I walked back from my weekly race with the overnight courier, I started to regret that I hadn't accepted Brian's invitation to dinner anyway. Yes, what Dave said was true—he might be acting nice to me just to throw me off. But my gut instinct told me that he was truly interested in me, at least a little. And if Dave could make a career out of trusting his gut instincts as often as he did, then I could at least trust mine once in a while. After all, we had a lot of the same genes, and therefore weren't my instincts as likely to be accurate as his?

I don't know what made me think of Brian all of a sudden. Watching other people enjoying the brisk, sunny fall afternoon on Main Street, I guess. A couple laughing together, friends window-shopping, a mother wiping ice cream off her son's freckled face. They were enjoying their time together.

I hadn't really enjoyed anyone's company, other than my children's, until I met Brian. With him, even burned food was funny, at least in retrospect. He was so easy about it.

I couldn't wait around hoping that the kids could occasionally fit me into their lives. I had to build a life of my own. And since Jeff and Linda took all my friends, I had to find new ones.

I could ask my neighbor Amy if she wanted to go to a movie or something. Or for a walk. That wasn't a bad idea; she seemed genuinely friendly.

But I'd been asked to dinner, and that seemed like an even better idea. If I could go back in time, I would change my answer to Brian's question.

Suddenly it seemed that everyone on the street was talking on a cell phone, and I wanted to call Brian. It would be rude to invite myself to dinner, but I could invite him over again.

When I turned the corner, though, away from the frivolity of Main Street and toward the plain houses and offices of Hill Street, reality sunk in. It was Tuesday afternoon. I only had three more workdays to figure out what was going on at the 1776 House before Dave arrived to show me up on Saturday. And all I could seem to think about was my social life, or lack thereof.

Dave had reminded me that I needed to consider what a potential thief would do with the stolen notes. If I could find them in someone's possession, well, that would make the case for certain.

If I were a TV investigator, I would have searched through all the suspects' houses by now. And what would I have found? Well, Paula probably would have destroyed the notes. Ann would have taken them to the DAP people. John would have sold them. Unless he needed to have them analyzed first to know their value. Patty would have stored them someplace safe until they could be analyzed. Brian never would have taken them. Probably. Or he, like Patty, would keep them safe until they could be analyzed. Probably.

Why hadn't they been analyzed yet, anyway? And what would that involve?

My workday was officially over after my drop-off at the overnight courier box, but that night, while the kids were working on their homework, I decided to take a lesson from them. I started my research on the Internet.

My first search under "artifact dating services" led to a bunch of online matchmaking Web sites. But once I refined my search, I learned that historic artifacts could be analyzed with X-rays, accelerator mass spectrometry, ion selective electrodes, microscopes, and cyclotrons. I didn't even know how to pronounce some of the words, much less understand what they involved. I would need to call a live person. I took down some phone numbers so I could call them the next day.

And while I was calling people, I would call Brian, too.

"Mom, why are you chewing on the phone cord?" Alicia's voice interrupted my mental planning session.

"I'm not." I quickly disentangled myself from the

cord and let it drop down next to the CD rack.

She reached over and picked up a length of cord. "I see bite marks."

"Really?" I leaned over to look. The evidence was particularly hard to deny, though I could probably blame the dog.

"You wrap the cord around your arm sometimes, and I think that stretches it too much," she said with a critical air. "But I've never seen you chew on it before. Is something wrong?"

"Wrong? No."

"Did Dad call? You stare at the phone like that after he's called."

"Your dad? No. No one called." She obviously misinterpreted my look this time, because I had no desire to pulverize the phone as I often did when Jeff called.

"See here?" She pointed to the junction where the phone cord connected with the receiver. "You've been pulling here. So you're probably thinking about someone you don't want to talk to."

I looked at her accusingly. "Are they teaching psychology in middle school now?"

She smiled. "*Teen Life* magazine."

"You're not a teen yet."

"So if it wasn't Dad," she persisted, her smile growing wider, "who was it? Who are you trying to avoid?"

"No one." That was the truth. I didn't want to avoid Brian; I wanted to see him, in fact. I wanted to call him. Or rather, I wanted him to call me.

She handed me the receiver. "Get it over with."

Her voice dropped to a whisper. "Is it the IRS?"

"No."

"Who, then?"

"Don't you have homework?"

She made a face but shuffled back toward the stairs, presumably either to do her homework in her room or to delve back into *Teen Life* so she could further analyze my anxieties.

The receiver was still in my hand. The phone book was on the desk shelf, within reach. And Ellicott City was a small enough town that he was the only Kieffer in the book.

He answered on the fourth ring, after I had already composed a message for the answering machine.

"Hello, Brian?" I winced at the sound of my voice, whiny and insecure.

"Yes." He paused. "Karen?"

"Um, yeah." *He recognized my voice! He sounds happy to talk to me!*

I clutched the receiver. *Why am I calling him again?*

There was silence for a few seconds while I tried to find words that fit together in some semblance of a sentence. "If you're still free on Saturday," I finally blurted out, "would you like to come over for dinner?"

"Oh, so you're—" His voice disappeared.

"Brian? Brian, are you there?" As I shook the receiver, the phone cord hit the floor. I had apparently pulled the cord so hard it disconnected and could only be thankful Alicia hadn't been there to witness it. I plugged the cord back in. "Hello?"

"You're back."

"Yeah, I, uh, did something to the. . ." I stopped before admitting my nervous habit, just in case he had been reading *Teen Life*, too. "So what were you saying? I missed most of it."

"Are you available Saturday? I thought you had plans with your kids."

"Well, it turns out I was wrong. I mean, turns out they had plans. But I don't."

"I think I understand." There was a smile in his voice. "So you can come to dinner with me?"

"You can come here," I put in quickly. I didn't want him to think I was forcing him to spend money on me.

"I have a special place in mind, and I asked you first, remember?"

I nodded. I had been remembering all week. Oh yeah, he couldn't see a nod. "Yes," I added belatedly.

"Good. I'll pick you up at six."

"Do you need directions?"

He laughed. "My memory isn't always what I'd like, but it's not that bad yet. I was just there last week."

It was last week. It seemed ages ago. "O–okay," I stammered, suddenly aware that one of the kids was coming down the stairs. "See you on Saturday."

## 15

Evan happened to catch a glimpse of himself in the bathroom mirror before we left for the 1776 House Saturday morning. He made a face. "I look like a hobbit."

"Well, so does everyone else there," I said quickly. "Your uncle Dave will look like an oversized hobbit." By reminding him that Dave was joining us, I hoped to keep Evan from getting too negative about the day. I had told him this would probably be the last time, and for once, it wasn't just one of those little white lies mothers tell to string along reluctant offspring. Though I really had made little progress with the case, Dave was coming out, and he would solve it. I couldn't decide if I was relieved or disappointed. Probably both. But for better or for worse, that would be the end of Saturdays at the 1776 House. I might have to go back next weekend to tie up loose ends, but Evan would be with his dad. So this was the last visit for him.

He actually looked quite cute in his gray breeches and big white shirt, with a pair of girl's white knee socks and black loafers. On his head he wore a man's broad-brimmed felt hat, which made him look even more like a little boy playing dress-up. I wouldn't have admitted that to him in a million years.

Alicia was trying to hem the rough edges of her apron/my bedsheet when I told her it was time to go.

"I thought Uncle Dave was coming."

"We'll meet him there." Secretly part of me was

hoping he wouldn't come, that some other case would get in the way. If I could just have one more week, I was sure I could learn something important that would lead to the thief. But right now Dave stood to take all the credit.

Dave's car was in the parking lot when we arrived, the black Thunderbird he drove when he was looking for attention rather than anonymity. And he greeted us in the gift shop with a big smile, looking for all the world like a jovial colonial innkeeper, complete with a pipe and tricorn hat. " 'Ow do I look?" he asked through teeth clutched around a thin white pipe stem. He tucked his hand into his lapel like George Washington posing for a portrait. "Pretty good, eh?"

Alicia ducked down in a move that was probably a curtsy. When she rose, she said, "Dearest Uncle, thee hast outfitted thyself admirably for the undertaking."

Dave's face wrinkled in confusion. "What?"

"Oh no." Evan took a step back into a shelf, knocking over a stack of colonial cookbooks. "Is she gonna be like that all day?"

"Most likely," I whispered to him as I tried to restack the cookbooks. "So we should get her to the kitchen as quickly as possible."

"Would thee escort me into the yard?" Alicia held out her arm to Dave. He looked at it for a moment as if unsure what to do with it.

"Go on." I nudged Dave toward her. "Alicia will show you around."

"Why are you talking in that weird way?" Evan asked his sister.

"I am a Quaker," she said dramatically, "not allowed to worship in my homeland and forced to come to the wilderness to toil for godless masters."

"I don't think Patty would care to hear herself described that way," I pointed out. "So be careful."

"Mother—r—r," she growled as she walked by me, "it's all part of the story. *She* understands." Alicia grabbed her uncle's arm and pulled him out the door to the yard.

That might buy me a little time. I could find Paula and work on her while Dave was listening to Patty and Alicia expound on their colonial personalities. But I had to do something with Evan first. "Can you help Brian again?" I asked him.

"Brian?"

"The blacksmith."

"Oh yeah, him. Yeah, sure, I guess." He cast a longing look at something resembling a cloth baseball on a shelf with wooden toys and other children's souvenirs.

"Remember, we'll be out of here after lunch today," I reminded him. "For your game."

He smiled as we headed over to Brian's shop.

Instead of the clang of metal on the anvil, we were greeted by the dull sound of an ax against wood. Brian was just outside the blacksmith shop, standing pieces of wood on a chopping block and cleaving them in two with an ax that looked like something an executioner might use. Okay, that was an exaggeration; it was more the device of an amateur executioner, someone who only lopped off heads in his spare time. But it was still a big, heavy, and dangerous-looking implement.

"Cool!" Evan ran toward him. "Can I try?"

I shook my head. "Absolutely no—" I stopped

when I caught a glimpse of Paula heading toward the kitchen. I wanted the chance to talk with her before Dave did. I turned a pleading look toward Brian. "Can he try that?"

Brian wiped sweat from his brow with the back of his hand. "Of course. He's apprenticed to me, remember. I won't—"

I turned to leave. "Great." I hated to cut him off, but I had to catch Paula before Dave did. If he talked to her for even a few minutes, he would figure out that she was the thief. I had to get her to confess to me before he got to her.

Paula had the usual frown on her face that I was coming to realize was not the mark of a mean personality but just an unfortunate tendency to dwell on things that made her mad. When I called her name, her face lit with a smile, so I knew her anger wasn't directed at me.

"I was wondering if I could work with you inside the house for a while today while my daughter's in the kitchen," I said. "I think it's better if I let her have a little space."

Paula nodded. "Good idea. If you were working in the yard, she might think you were spying on her."

"Exactly." I nodded, although the thought never would have occurred to me.

"We're making final preparations for the DAP visit," Paula said as she started briskly for the house. "So we can use all the help we can get."

My heart or some other organ jumped into my throat, making it suddenly difficult to breathe. "Is that next Saturday?" Mrs. McGregor wanted the notes before that visit.

"A few days after. The site manager will stop by on Tuesday, and then the whole entourage descends on Wednesday."

I followed her through the door that led to the main part of the house. "Are you nervous?" I sure was. I mean, I expected Dave to wind up the case if I couldn't, but what if he failed? Then the whole agency would have failed.

"Nervous, no. Disappointed, yes. Who stacked those boxes there?" With a frown, she marched over to a stack of small cardboard boxes underneath the far corner of a table in the hall.

I hurried after her. "Well, I bet you're glad the Washington notes are gone."

She waved that away. "Those I could have covered with a quilt or something when Eileen wasn't looking. But I can't very well throw a blanket over the woman herself."

"Throw a blanket over. . ."

"She insists on wearing that ridiculous yellow polyester gown that she made for the bicentennial. With a shower cap on her head. And she'll be in every picture, I guarantee it. She and Ann fawn all over those ridiculous DAP people."

"If they're ridiculous, why do you care what they think of the site?"

She sighed as she bent down to examine the boxes. "They control a lot of grant money. We're hoping to restore the stable, and we sure could use their help, with state money being so scarce." She opened a box and frowned. "Commemorative Christmas ornaments. More junk for the gift shop."

I tried to steer the conversation back on track before she could start ranting about the period-incorrect glass balls. "Do you think they would have wanted to see the Washington notes?"

"I'm sure they expect to. Eileen said she hasn't told them they're missing. She keeps saying, 'They'll turn up,' as if we'd just misplaced them or something. As if they hadn't spent every afternoon for a week combing through the house and grounds."

"What do you think *really* happened to them?"

"I don't know. I was just so pleased, I decided not to look a gift horse in the mouth." She scooped the boxes into her arms and stood.

"Do you think one of the volunteers stole them? Weren't you near the room at the time they went missing? Who do you remember seeing in the house at the time?"

She gave me a quizzical look. "Who are you, Perry Mason?"

I forced a laugh. "No, it just strikes me as odd, that's all. That the site's number one claim to fame should disappear right before this important visit. It seems as if someone deliberately wanted the notes out of sight."

"The notes aren't the site's best claim to fame," Paula called over her shoulder as she headed toward the gift shop. "We are the best representation of a middle-class home and business establishment in this whole region. We should be proud of what we are, not what we wish we were."

"So you wanted the notes out of sight."

"Sure did." She paused to readjust the boxes in her arms.

I caught up with her and lowered my voice. "And you were in the house at the time they were taken."

She nodded. "Most likely."

I was hoping she'd confess here, but she didn't. I licked my lips. "What would you say if someone suggested that *you'd* taken the notes?"

"Someone *did* suggest it. Eileen McGregor accused me right to my face."

"And what did you say?"

"I said I wish I'd thought of it. But it never occurred to me to simply remove the worthless things from the case. I'm glad it occurred to someone else, though."

"Even if they've been sold away or destroyed?"

"Anyone who could sell that rubbish deserves credit for the effort."

I started to ask where she was on the night of the theft, but then I remembered that she had already confessed to being right here at the time. She had motive and no alibi. What she lacked was a guilty conscience, but then, if she felt herself justified, she would see no reason to feel guilty.

She looked no closer to confessing than she had at the start of our conversation.

"Whoever stole them might go to jail," I said softly.

"No!" The boxes tumbled from her arms. Her gaze shifted briefly to the window facing the yard. "There's no proof the notes were of any value. I can't believe the police would put someone in jail for that."

"Mrs. McGregor told me they were insured for twenty-five thousand dollars." I made that up. I hadn't even asked if they'd been insured, but it would have been a really good question, and I would ask as soon as I had the chance.

"Twenty-five thousand dollars?" Her face looked even paler than usual under her black silk hat. She definitely seemed uneasy now, but her frequent glances toward the window made it appear that she was worried for someone out there rather than for herself.

She looked in the direction of the blacksmith shop far too many times.

This would have been so much easier if she had just confessed! Instead, she *almost* acted as though she thought Brian might be responsible.

As we bent down to retrieve the boxes, I saw something flash by along the floorboards. "Was that a mouse?"

Paula's gaze followed mine for a moment. "Probably. They always get in this time of year."

I repressed a shiver of revulsion. "Well, you'd better get Patty's cat up here before the DAP photographers spot it."

"Why?" Paula looked very relieved at the change of subject. "Mice are period correct. We should probably import mice. And besides," she added as she straightened up, "Patty doesn't have a cat."

<hr />

*If Patty doesn't have a cat, then why did she tell me it was her cat's name on that paper I found?* The obvious answer was that she had lied to me. Why? What was there about that name that made her feel the need to lie about it?

And what *was* the name? I couldn't even remember it. It was one of those Greek or Roman gods, like Zeus, but that wasn't it.

I charged out of the house ready to ask Patty about it, but then I couldn't decide. Maybe I should wait, come up with a strategy.

Maybe I should tell Dave and let *him* come up with a strategy. He was, after all, the expert. I was so concerned about trying to get credit for myself that I really hadn't considered the good of the client at all. Mrs. McGregor hired us to find the notes before the DAP visit. If I could help Dave find the notes now, I needed to do it, even if he took all the credit. It would be better for the client and for the whole firm.

I found Dave sitting in the yard near the black-smith shop, his hand wrapped in a bloodstained handkerchief.

I ran over to him. "What happened?"

"It's nothing, no need to panic." He grinned.

I sat down next to him, grateful that the only other people in the yard were a family posing a Flat Stanley for pictures wearing a tricorn hat from the gift shop. "I'm panicked about something else," I confessed in a low voice. "The big daughters-of-the-patriots group is coming soon, so we've got to get the notes back *this week*."

Dave looked around for a moment as if taking mental inventory. "And your suspects are this Holbrock who isn't here, the lady in the gift shop, the sisters, and the blacksmith?"

"Yes." I was whispering but trying to whisper loudly enough for him to hear me over the sounds of some suddenly noisy birds in a nearby tree. "I think it was one of the sisters. Patty lied to me and said she has a cat when she really doesn't."

"And why would Patty steal the notes?"

"To get them out of the way."

He rubbed his hand against his jaw. "But there was the second theft, the money. Would she take that?"

"I—I don't know."

Dave looked around again. "You told me the other suspect, John, had a history. And he was working with the money that was stolen."

"He was," I admitted. I really didn't think he would take the money, but I couldn't explain why. Then I remembered. "But it was Patty who suggested that he help me at the table. It wasn't his idea."

Dave pursed his lips. "Could be significant." The look in his eyes, however, indicated that he thought just the opposite. "And how about the blacksmith, Kieffer? Was he near the money?"

"I don't think so."

"And why is he a suspect in the theft of the notes?"

"Because he had motive and opportunity".

"And his motive?"

"He wanted the notes out of the way, too."

Dave shook his head. "That just doesn't seem like enough grounds to me. I think it had to be Holbrock."

"You do?"

"Nine times out of ten, it'll be the guy with the obvious motive. Remember that. Motive is never proof in court, but it will lead to proof—I guarantee it."

I felt a weight lift off my chest. "So you don't think Brian is guilty?"

"Brian?" He followed my gaze. "Oh, the blacksmith. No, probably not, if you don't." Dave glanced at his wrist, at the place where his watch would be if he hadn't taken it off. "Do you think this Holbrock will show today?"

"If he's not here by now, probably not. But he might. He's come late before."

With a huff, Dave pushed himself up to a standing position. "All right, then, you watch for him here while I see if I can find him at home."

"We have to leave at 1:00 to get ready for Evan's game."

"I'll find him myself, then," Dave offered with a reassuring smile. "Don't worry about it. It's not really your job, anyway."

I was probably supposed to smile back, but I wasn't exactly cheered by his reminder that he considered me little more than a secretary. This was apparently not only my first case, but my last one, too. He had taken over.

He patted the spot at his waist where his cell phone would be holstered if he wasn't dressed like a hobbit. "Call me if he shows up before you leave."

"I will."

He held open his coat. "And you can bring these clothes back for me later, right?"

"You're leaving in them?"

"I can change in the car."

"You're driving a convertible."

"Stop trying to be Mom, okay?" He waved toward the kitchen. "Go be *their* mom. Watch your daughter play Juliet in the kitchen and admire your boy as he splits wood and then go cheer his soccer team to victory. Have fun. I'll see you Monday." He stalked around the side of the house toward the parking lot.

I should have felt relieved. He didn't see any reason to think Brian was guilty, so I shouldn't either. I shouldn't worry about the expression on Paula's face as she looked out at the blacksmith shop. Dave had considered the case, read my progress reports, evaluated the suspects. And he would confront the one he felt was guilty. He was the expert, so he was probably right in thinking John was guilty. It was probably the most common scenario, someone stealing an article to sell it for a personal profit.

But in my time at the site, I had learned that some people are motivated by much more than money. The dedicated volunteers all wanted to share the site's history with the public; they just disagreed about the best way to accomplish this goal. Dave didn't understand their dedication.

And I was about to go out with perhaps the most dedicated one of all.

## 16

The doorbell rang while I was still deciding what to wear. I debated sending the dog out front for a while to keep Brian busy while I threw on some fresh clothes, but instead just replaced my soccer mom T-shirt with a sweater set and ran downstairs, still wearing jeans.

"Hi," I said breathlessly as I opened the door.

He squinted at me. "I always have the feeling I'm catching you in the middle of running a marathon."

"No, I just had to run downstairs from the. . ." I let the words trail off as he stepped inside. It was only a few feet from the bedroom to the stairs to the door. I really shouldn't be out of breath like this. I held the door open. "Don't worry; she's in the backyard."

"The dog or your daughter?"

"Both." I smiled. "No, actually, Alicia is at a party. I think. Unless I sent the wrong one." I peered out through a window to the backyard, hoping he would laugh at my joke.

He did.

"Hey, I didn't really have time to change after the game." I omitted the fact that I lacked time only because I stared at my closet for twenty minutes without reaching a decision. "Is it okay to wear jeans to this restaurant?"

"Sure. It's a very casual place."

"Oh, good." I hoped it wasn't one of those Mexican places where they put a giant sombrero on your head

190 George Washington Stepped Here

and make you stand in your chair if it's even remotely close to your birthday.

He nodded toward the door. "Are you ready?"

"I guess I am, then." I checked to make sure the dog had water in her bowl and turned on the porch light. I was going *out*.

Me.

I hoped one of the neighbors was watching.

The easy joking attitude we'd shared at the house evaporated when we were sitting next to each other in the cab of Brian's pickup truck. He suddenly seemed very close and very large and powerful. I felt like a bowl of Jell-O.

He drove toward Main Street, and I tried to guess which restaurant might be our destination. Then he turned off and drove up a steep hill. I thought there were only houses up on top of the hill, and maybe a church.

I wanted to ask where we were going, but my tongue seemed to be stuck to the roof of my mouth.

"Are you beginning to wonder where we're headed?" he asked with a nervous grin.

I nodded.

"We're almost there."

Were we going to a relative's house? Was he going to have his mother cook for me? The houses we passed were Victorian, not as stately as most because of the odd ways they were nestled into the hill on one side of the street or hanging off the edge of the hill on the other side.

I hoped his mother was not too judgmental.

But as the winding street uncurled in front of us

for the last time, we stopped in front of not a Victorian house but a stone church with a large brick building behind it. The parking lot was about two-thirds full, with families walking toward the door.

"Are we going to church first?" I asked nervously. I knew some people who stopped to say prayers before meals, so maybe there were people who went to church before they went out to dinner.

"We are going to church *for* dinner." Brian jumped out, and before I could ask my next question, he had come around to open the door for me. "To the Multicultural Café."

"No sushi, right?" I joked. "You promised you wouldn't make me eat raw fish." I hoped I looked calm, because on the inside I was practically screaming. *What kind of a date is this? Who takes a girl out to church for dinner? What are we going to eat, four courses of Communion wafers?*

I slid out of the seat to the ground. It was a long way down, and I landed with a very ungraceful *thud.*

As we walked toward the brick building behind the church (so maybe it wouldn't be Communion wafers, after all), Brian's hand swung very close to my own. A couple of times it looked as if he would have taken my hand, so we'd be holding hands like on a date, which would have appealed to me before, but now that we were at a church, it seemed all wrong. This was too weird, and I couldn't wait until it was over.

When he held the door open for me, I had to fight the urge to say, "No, thank you." Instead, I went in.

Sounds of voices and laughter came from a set of stairs leading down to our right. There were giant paper flowers taped everywhere, and bright garlands and signs in other languages that probably said things like, "Welcome," and "Good food here," but my skill with foreign language had never been very strong, so the signs could have said, "Try the roast bat" and "Raw fish is great with ketchup."

Brian waved toward the stairs. "After you."

I clutched the railing and started down. After a few seconds, I realized I was stepping in time with odd jungle music. By the time we reached the bottom, it seemed pretty dark, and I half expected to see vines and snakes hanging from the ceiling.

"Konbanwa." A blond girl in a kimono bowed.

I immediately looked around to see if anybody appeared to be dining on raw fish. The vast, dark space was divided into separate sections, each decorated with a different theme.

With a coy smile on her face, the young hostess led us to a section in the darkest part of the room. Less exotic than some of the other areas, our corner was decorated with candles and posters to resemble an Italian bistro. As if on cue, the music changed to a soft ballad crooned by a tenor whom I assumed to be Italian. We passed three high school–aged boys who stood in a cluster comparing notes on pads. They stopped and stared.

"Aren't you guys supposed to be working for tips?" Brian called over his shoulder.

They grinned. "I get Brian's table," one of them announced as he followed us.

"Not if I get there first." Another one dodged around several tables to get ahead of us. He pointed to a table in the corner. "That one."

The hostess nodded. She led us to a table decorated with two dripping candles and a handful of mums in a jar of water. After she placed two sheets of paper on the table, she bowed again. "Enjoy your dinner, Brian." She winked before walking away with tiny steps.

Brian and I both took hold of the same chair. "I got it first," I said with a nervous laugh.

"I was going to hold it for you, actually."

"Oh." I felt my face flush to the roots of my hair. It had been so long since someone had held a chair for me that I'd forgotten the practice entirely.

The pieces of paper the hostess had set down on the table were menus, and I stared at mine long enough to memorize it, because for some reason I really didn't want to look at Brian. The menu offered a Japanese meal (no fish, either raw or cooked), an Italian meal, Ethiopian dishes, and Mexican/Cuban selections. I read it through about seven times before Brian broke the silence.

He cleared his throat. "I'm sorry if you're disappointed."

"I'm not," I said quickly. Okay, that wasn't true. Part of that weird feeling in my gut was disappointment. And probably some annoyance. I had hoped for a romantic date, and instead he had taken me to church. "I'm just surprised, that's all." I finally looked up at him. And then I wished I hadn't spent so much time staring at a piece of Xeroxed paper.

An anxious frown pulled his mouth down at the corners. Worry lines creased his forehead. He seemed to be about the most miserable man in existence at that moment. And I had the distinct impression that it was my fault.

I set down my menu. "What's wrong?"

"Do you want to leave?" He gripped the edge of the table.

"Leave? We just got here."

He looked down. "This was a bad idea."

I didn't know what to say to that. My first thought was to reassure him that no, it was a great idea. But I honestly didn't think it was. "I think you should have told me," I finally said.

He gave a wistful smile. "I thought it might be a funny surprise."

"Well, it was a more of an annoying surprise." But to be fair, I had to admit it would be funny to talk about later. The expression on my face when we pulled into the parking lot probably rivaled that of a prizewinning largemouth bass.

I glanced around. The three boys who had stared at us when we came in were now watching us again, nudging each other, and laughing. "And somebody thinks it's funny." I waved toward the boys. "I take it you know these kids?"

He nodded. "My youth group. They're hosting this dinner to raise funds for the summer mission trip."

"Mission trip? Like to Africa or something?" The word *mission* made me think of a blustering Englishman in a pith helmet handing out Bibles to illiterate natives.

"They'd love to go to Africa, but that's a little out of our reach, I'm afraid. We're hoping to go to an Indian reservation in South Dakota."

"What will you do?"

"Visit, do some repair work on some of the houses, and teach a week of the summer school program."

I looked at the boys for a minute. "That sounds pretty neat, actually. Like you're doing something useful."

He laughed. "That's the idea. We need to be God's hands in the world."

"I never thought of it that way." The church my parents made me attend sometimes when I was a kid never sent people on mission trips or talked about being God's hands. They just talked about praying and rules.

And the church never pretended it was a restaurant, either.

The music changed to something like the Mexican Hat Dance. A group of girls filed into the room with roses in their teeth, stomping their feet and swishing big colorful skirts. They shuffled around the room, occasionally twirling and shouting, "Olé!" Then they left, as suddenly as they'd entered, but with much more giggling.

Brian smiled. "A preview of the show."

"There's a show?"

"Oh yes. They've been practicing for weeks. What they lack in talent they make up for in enthusiasm."

"It does seem like they're having a lot of fun." I looked around again. The three boys had dispersed and were now taking orders or serving food to families and couples at tables throughout the room. A door opened nearby to reveal a stainless-steel kitchen full of teens who were cooking a little and laughing a lot.

No one was wearing a tie. In fact, most people

were dressed as if they were going to the movies or the mall.

"This is pretty informal for a church," I marveled.

He grinned. "We're pretty informal people."

It didn't seem much like a church at all, in fact.

Brian nodded to someone behind me, and before I knew it, our table was surrounded by the three gangly teen waiters clamoring to take our orders. They finally agreed that one of them would write down the order and the other two would bring the food.

"I'll have the Japanese meal." Brian handed his menu to one of the boys.

"Oh, don't get that one," he advised. "It's all frozen food, and they're not cooking it long enough and the vegetables have ice crystals in the middle."

"Cuban?" Brian asked.

The boy shook his head. "Jane dropped her headband in the refried beans, and we haven't found it yet."

Brian made a face. "What do you suggest, then?"

One of the other boys leaned over him. "Ooh, the Ethiopian is good."

Brian nodded. "I'll have that."

They all turned to me expectantly. "Has anyone dropped anything in the spaghetti?" I probably shouldn't have asked, because I was going to order it anyway. All the others were a little too exotic for my taste.

The waiter shook his head. "Not yet. And the garlic bread's really great."

I handed him the menu. "I'll take it. And I'll try not to breathe in your general direction." I smiled at Brian, struck by the sudden realization that it was the first time I had smiled since we left the house.

The boys laughed. "I think the Ethiopian has lots of garlic, too," one of them added as he left the table. "So you'll cancel each other out." He winked at Brian.

It looked to me as though Brian was turning red, but it was hard to tell in the dim light. The music changed to some sort of techno-pop music that I guessed was supposed to sound Japanese.

I looked at a poster of the Leaning Tower of Pisa. "It doesn't really fit, somehow."

We both laughed. And suddenly it seemed much easier to look at Brian. And to talk.

Brian told me about the group, the various kids, and which ones would be heading off for college soon. After this dinner, their next big project would be a play about a group of disgruntled toys who try to find the real meaning of Christmas.

Our food arrived in good time, and I found no unexpected hair accessories in my spaghetti sauce.

Suddenly the dim lights grew even dimmer. "La–a–a–dies and gentleme–e–e–n," a boy's voice boomed excitedly over a loudspeaker, "we have an important announcement to make. Our fearless leader, Brian, has actually got a *date* for the evening. This may be a sign that the end of the world is at hand."

I could feel my face heat up as laughter rang out on all sides. Brian squeezed my hand.

"Welcome to the Multicultural Café. We will now entertain you with performers from all over the world. Our first act is. . ." There was a rustling of paper. "He's not ready? Oh, okay. Then our first act will be. . .Jake and His Gargling Rabbits."

"Where are they from?" someone from the audience asked in a loud voice.

"I think Jake's from Ohio," the announcer said uncertainly.

"That's not international."

"They're not real rabbits, either." The curtain rustled on the side and a hand held up a stuffed purple rabbit. "Look, I think this one was made in Taiwan." He dangled it by the tag.

Everyone laughed again. Another hand came out and snatched the rabbit back behind the curtain.

The gargling stuffed rabbits turned out to be one of the more entertaining acts of the evening. But they were all pretty funny, and it wasn't until the end of the show that I remembered that we were in a church. After the last act, Brian went up to the stage.

He smiled as his eyes scanned the audience. "I'd like to thank all of you for coming." Then he turned to his cast of performers and servers, his group. "Well, most of you. Some of you I could have done without."

They laughed.

"In all seriousness, though," Brian continued, "your support allows us to do great things, and we appreciate it. I'd like to close the evening now with a prayer."

My hands clenched in my lap. Prayer? Right now? When we were having so much fun?

"Dear Lord," he said in a steady voice, "we thank You for this opportunity to come together in fellowship, and we thank You for the support we've received for the work of our church and this group. Keep us mindful of Your will for us. And keep us safe until we meet again. In Jesus' name we pray. . ."

"Amen," everyone responded in unison. Everyone but me, that is. I didn't know it was time to yet. Prayers in church could go on forever, if I remembered correctly.

As I was wondering what we were supposed to say next, I realized that everyone was chatting among themselves and chairs were scraping against the floor as people stood to leave. It was over. So apparently not all prayers dragged on past the point where people stopped listening.

"I'm sorry about all the attention," Brian apologized as we stepped outside into the parking lot. "I should have expected it, but I didn't. I hope it didn't embarrass you too badly."

"It didn't." I smiled. "I think they intended to embarrass *you*."

"That they did. But I wasn't sure how it would make you feel. Especially since you looked so unhappy when we got here. . ." His words trailed off as he looked away from me. "It was probably a mistake. To throw you in the middle of this so suddenly. I guess I just thought it would be fun."

I put a hand on his arm to stop him. "It *was* fun. I have to admit I wasn't sure when we got here. You know, church and all."

He looked at me with concern. "You don't like church."

I shrugged. "It's not a matter of liking it, really. It's just that it's church. Prayers and rules and stuff. Not exactly an ideal date."

"Well, no." He smiled gently. "That wouldn't have been."

"But this wasn't what I expected. It was. . .fun." I smiled as Brian held open the door for me. If I thought it was a long way down from the seat to the ground, it seemed twice as far to haul myself back up there. I reached out for the door just as Brian was shutting it for me.

"Watch your fingers!" he warned. He was shaking his head as he walked around the truck and got in on the driver's side. "I was afraid I was going to be the cause of two bloody injuries in your family today."

The look I gave him must have been as blank as my memory.

"Your brother?" he prompted. "I forgot to ask you how he was doing. Did he have a long wait in the emergency room?"

"What happened to my brother?"

"At the House. Evan was demonstrating how to split wood, and when your brother took a turn, he got the ax jammed in the wood. He split his hand open trying to get it loose. He left right after that, so I assumed he went to get stitches."

Now I remembered the bloody handkerchief wrapped around Dave's hand. "I didn't realize it was that bad. But it doesn't matter, as long as he didn't actually chop off his hand entirely. He'd never wait in the ER."

Brian shook his head. "Bad judgment, then."

"That would be Dave for you," I agreed.

Dave was my brother. I had known him all my life, and I knew that sometimes he could exhibit appallingly bad judgment. The decision to pitch a tent on the roof of our high school during senior week, for example. . .

Now that I was working for him, though, I was

required to trust that questionable judgment. It was his company; he had the final say.

But that didn't always make him right.

The taillights of cars streaming out of the parking lot coalesced into a long streak of red as I let my eyes go out of focus.

I didn't think Dave was right.

Patty's suspicious behavior in regard to that name had more meaning than Dave realized. Whether she was covering something for herself or someone else, she was hiding something. I had to find out what that name meant.

As soon as I remembered what it was.

## 17

Alicia bounded through the door all jubilant and starry-eyed almost as soon as I had said good night to Brian and watched his truck lights disappear down the street. So reflections on my evening and Patty's mysterious name and asking Brian over again were pushed aside while Alicia and I snuggled on the couch with a bowl of popcorn and two Diet Cokes. She told me all about the party, how she was afraid to skate in front of people but did better than she thought she would. Who fell, who got pushed, and how many of the boys were cute. I didn't understand it all (she once referred to someone's shoes as "crispy"), but I enjoyed it nevertheless. She shared more with me in that evening than she had for the previous two months, and I started to wonder if letting her go on her own more might enable us to become closer.

After the popcorn with movie theater butter and our custom pancakes the next morning, I decided I needed an extra walk and so did the dog, who not only cleaned up the pieces of dropped popcorn but also helped herself to the first plate of pancakes while my back was turned. Alicia was instant messaging friends about the party. Evan wouldn't be dropped off for another hour or two, so Tara and I would be walking on our own.

The air had the feel of autumn to it—not cold yet, but crisp and dry, with the sense of impending change. Red and orange leaves cascaded to the ground with each gust of wind. It seemed to carry a "seize the day" message, urging enjoyment of each moment before winter removed the light, heat, and color from the world.

It was a pretty day to walk with a friend.

It would have been nice to *have* a friend to invite. I missed my old neighbors, even though they had been Linda's friends more than mine.

I dragged Tara over to Amy's house and rang the bell.

She answered the door with a dish towel in her hand and big fluffy cat slippers on her feet.

"I was wondering if you might want to join me for a walk." My neighborly smile faltered a bit when I realized that Tara was digging up a chrysanthemum next to the porch. I yanked the leash to pull her over to the other side.

"A walk? Sure." Amy tossed the dish towel in the general direction of the kitchen. "Oh, wait. I need shoes."

I peered through the screen. "I have some like that. Slippers shaped like animals."

She grinned. "Mother's Day. From my daughter."

"I got mine from my son. It gets worse when they discover costume jewelry."

She pulled out a pair of sneakers. "Oh yeah?"

"I've got one pair of earrings with stones the size of the Hope Diamond and about three times as heavy." I raised my voice in imitation of a young Alicia. "Why don't you wear those, Mommy? They're so pretty!"

She laughed. "I don't think Nicole can see the jewelry counter yet. But it's only a matter of time. Do I need a jacket?"

"No, it's beautiful out."

We walked in silence for a few minutes until we came to the end of the street and had to decide which way to go.

"This way?" Amy leaned toward the left.

I was about to turn right as I always did. Toward the west. Away from our old neighborhood, where Jeff still lived with Linda. "Um, yeah, I guess."

"We can go the other way if you want," she said quickly, obviously sensing my unease.

"It doesn't matter," I lied.

"Well there's a street down this way lined with sugar maples, and they should still have leaves at this point."

"Good idea," I lied again. It actually wasn't a bad idea—for her. The street she referred to was indeed beautiful this time of year when the leaves glowed with red and orange tones that were almost fluorescent. But I didn't want to see it.

I had driven past that street every day of my married life. That life was over and I wanted no reminders. It was time to make my new life worth living.

I glanced over at Amy. "I'm sorry I've been so grumpy."

She laughed. "You haven't been grumpy."

"I have," I insisted. "Whenever you talk to me. I haven't been very nice."

"Well, you're nice now."

"I just wanted you to know it wasn't you. It was me." I stared at Tara's leash for a moment, my gaze following the leather line from my hand until it became lost in a tangle of dark fur at her neck. "I had a neighbor who went bad on me, but it was silly to think that all neighbors would be like that."

"Went bad? Like postal or something?"

I laughed, picturing Linda in her high heels and tight pants brandishing a toy machine gun in the local post office. Then I stopped laughing. If I was going to make Amy understand why I had been so rude, I should explain the whole thing. And I had learned the other night, talking with Brian, that sharing the story made it easier, not harder, to bear. "It was almost as bad. She had an affair with my husband." I waited to see whether she would look as if there were something wrong with me.

Amy's eyes doubled in size behind her wire-rimmed glasses. "Really?"

I nodded, inwardly cringing at the sense of satisfaction I gained from her sympathetic look of horror.

"So what did you do?" she asked breathlessly.

"Well, looking back on it now, I figure I may have unintentionally gotten the best possible revenge. I let her have him."

She grinned. "Ha! I hope they made each other miserable."

"Actually," I sighed, "I think they're pretty happy together. She has two kids from an earlier marriage, and they get along pretty well with Evan and Alicia when they visit."

"How often is that?"

"Every other weekend and one night a week."

She smiled. "So you get some time off from being a mom."

"Yeah, whether I want it or not." I stopped to disentangle Tara from an ugly evergreen shrub.

"Sorry." Amy put her hand on my arm. "I hadn't

thought of it that way. I was just thinking how hard it is to find a babysitter."

"That's okay. You know. . ." I started to walk again. "I like the idea that Linda and Jeff are forced to provide babysitting for me every other weekend."

"Unpaid."

"That's right. Free babysitting. I could go to Acapulco for the weekend with no problem."

"You should."

"Well, I'm actually not sure I'd want to. And I don't have the money. But at least I know I *could*." I felt a new sense of freedom.

That lasted for at least thirty seconds until I realized I could no longer move forward because the dog had now wrapped her leash around a deer statue in someone's yard.

She sniffed at it and growled.

I untangled the leash. "C'mon Tara. It's not a cat. It's not even a deer." I turned to Amy. "I'm surprised she didn't growl at your slippers. Two cats almost within her reach."

The image of the pink whiskered slippers had stayed in my mind all during our walk, and I couldn't for the life of me figure out why. But when I said the word "cat" this last time, I remembered. Patty's cat. Or lack thereof. I had a mystery to solve.

"Do you mind if we head back?" I asked. "I need to do some work."

---

I found a chart of Greek and Roman gods online and tried to decide which one, if any, Patty had written on that sheet of paper. The paper that she burned.

*Adonis, Aphrodite, Apollo, Artemis, Athena.* I kind of thought it started with *A*.

Had she or Paula given the Washington notes to someone with that name? Sold them? Stored them? Burned them? Apollo was the god of the sun. Her note could be a cryptic way of telling someone that she'd burned the notes.

Maybe Patty's note had nothing to do with the missing artifact. But what about the missing money?

I looked at the list of names again. She wouldn't burn up the money.

But she wouldn't take the money, either. She loved the site, so why would she steal much-needed revenue?

I was almost grateful when Evan came home and complained that he had no clean socks. Laundry I knew I could handle. Clothes in the washer, then in the dryer, then folded and put away. Something accomplished. But I could spend the rest of the day staring at the list of Greek names and make no progress whatsoever.

It was raining on Wednesday when Jeff came to pick up the kids, so he had the top up and his convertible looked decidedly less sporty.

"You'd better take an umbrella." I handed the longest one I could find to Evan. "And be careful that you don't accidentally poke it through the top of the car. Those soft tops can be pretty fragile."

I once heard that you shouldn't use the word "don't" with children because it subtly encourages them to do just the thing you are trying to prohibit. I didn't know if the metal end of an umbrella would really make a hole in the top of Jeff's car, but it was worth a shot.

Both kids lumbered out into the rain with umbrellas big enough to cover a golf cart. Now I could concentrate on dinner. I had invited Brian over again to prove that I could fix a decent meal without burning, dropping, or spilling most of it. I hadn't burned so much as a toast crumb all week.

But as I got the bottle of Sesame Goddess salad dressing out of the refrigerator, I thought about the list of Greek and Roman names again.

Was Patty's note a cryptic shopping list?

*What did the name mean?*

I stared at the bottle labeled with a picture of a curvy young woman brandishing a head of lettuce.

Instead of trying to figure out what the name could lead to, I should see what other things might lead to that name. Other than salad dressing, because I really didn't think that was it and it didn't start with an *A* anyway.

I went to the computer and started searching for information about auctions of historic artifacts. Maybe a buyer or someone who represented a buyer might have one of the names from my *A* list. But, of course, once I started searching, I realized that all bidders were identified online by numbers only, and none of the auction houses started with *A* or even had vaguely Greek-sounding names.

The doorbell rang.

When I glanced toward the front door, I could see that it had grown dark outside.

And there was a burning smell coming from the kitchen.

I shoved the dog into the backyard.

"You won't believe this," I said as I opened the front door for Brian.

He sniffed. "Should I order a pizza?"

"Probably." I went to the kitchen to check, but the smell alone made it pretty obvious that my sausage and pepper lasagna was going to be inedible. I took it out of the oven sadly. All that freshly grated Parmesan cheese charred to a leathery slab.

The smoke alarm went off.

"Would you like to go out?" Brian asked as I came back. "I promise to take you to a real restaurant this time."

I shook my head. "It's raining. Let's make the pizza guy go out." As long as he didn't drive a convertible.

We settled down in the living room to talk while we waited for the delivery, and this time I was determined not to cry, because I know it makes my nose really red.

Brian sat closer to me than he had last time, or maybe I just wanted him to sit closer since he wasn't probing for information about my past life. We talked about the church talent show and Alicia's drama classes and Evan's ability to do his spelling homework while simultaneously destroying an island of mutant dinosaurs in a video game. An amusing discussion. And very safe.

The pizza arrived right on schedule, and though the box was dripping with rain (maybe the delivery guy *did* drive a convertible), the pizza was fine. I ate two pieces with onion and sausage and then tried to swallow a horrifying belch.

Judging by Brian's laughter, I didn't succeed in my quest for discretion.

I winced as I caught a whiff of my own breath. "There was more garlic on this than I realized."

"At least we'll 'cancel each other out,' as Jesse said Saturday."

I felt my face flush. The waiter's remark seemed to hint that Brian and I would be close enough that breath would be a big issue. That to me meant either that we would be shouting in each other's faces or that we would kiss. I didn't think either one was likely, but just the thought made me blush. Brian was probably thinking of me as a great colonial trainee or a possible assistant leader for a church project. I was thinking of him as a boyfriend.

"Um, do you want some more soda?" I stood up, resolving to stick my face in the freezer on a nice long hunt for ice cubes.

"I'm good, thanks." He sat back against the cushions.

It actually did take me awhile to find ice, because the kids and I never take time to make any. But I eventually found an old tray in the back of the freezer with cubes shaped like pouncing velociraptors.

I bit the head off one and sucked on the cool freshness, but my garlic breath returned as soon as the dinosaur head was gone.

What else might erase the sour garlic taste in my mouth? Parsley. I rummaged through the vegetable drawer of the fridge, but the only herb I found was chives, and I doubted that would help much.

"Are you okay?" Brian called from the other room.

I realized I was spending more of the evening with a major kitchen appliance than with him. Breath notwithstanding, I took myself and the melting velociraptors back into the living room.

I wasn't quite sure where to sit. If I sat where I had before, it would seem as if I was practically throwing myself on his lap.

"Are you sure you're okay?" Brian's forehead wrinkled with concern.

That made me laugh. "Yes." I sat back down exactly where I had been before.

"Do I make you nervous?" he said suddenly.

I laughed again, but it was nerves more than amusement this time. "Yes, sometimes."

"Good." He sighed with relief.

"You want to make me nervous?"

Now he looked confused. "No, that's not it. It's just that you—and I—and I like to talk to you, but sometimes. . ." He raked his hand through his hair. "I don't know, it just gets hard to talk all of a sudden."

"But other times it's easy."

"Exactly."

Neither of us said anything for a while. Rain beat down in a heavy staccato on the back deck. The scent of the storm fluttered through the air on the breeze from a window I had cracked open. It was a clean smell, like the world smelled when it was new and before people had discovered how to use coal and rubber.

Brian shifted his position just slightly, but it was enough to draw my attention right back to the couch and the realization of just how close we were sitting. I wanted to snuggle next to him and lay my head on his shoulder. But I still felt I hardly knew him. So I just looked at him instead.

And then I had to look away. Because he was staring at me with an intensity that I could not match. He leaned closer, and then I could picture the scene as a movie, where I was watching an actress playing my role. He would lift my chin and kiss me, very slowly, very hesitantly. And the lighting would be soft and the music would beat just like the rain outside.

Instead, he backed away.

When I realized the movie scene was never going to play out, I looked back up at him.

His whole body was tense, his mouth tight-lipped, and his eyes held an expression of deep anguish and something akin to guilt. When he realized I was watching him, he looked away.

This time it was my turn to ask him. "Are you okay?"

He shook his head. "I like you, Karen. And it doesn't seem fair to her."

I knew he meant the pretty woman at the spinning wheel. His wife, Chloe.

"You don't talk about her much." I meant this to come out as a question, but as I said the words, I knew them to be a simple statement of truth.

"It—I keep her all to myself. If I talk about her, I'm sharing her with others."

"You're afraid to lose her?"

"Yes." He gave me a broken smile.

I felt woefully inadequate and didn't know what to say. No one close to me had died. What could I possibly think of to say that others had not said before, and much better? I couldn't even offer a hug, because that would make him feel disloyal.

But he seemed to hurt so much, I had to try to find something to say.

"It seems to me," I said finally, "that you're just holding on to a lot of pain. You're keeping all of it, and you're not sharing, but what you're keeping hurts so much you feel only the loss. You can't remember the happy times."

"The happy times." His face grew sullen. "Sometimes I think they're gone forever."

"That's not fair to her," I said softly. "She tried to keep her life, but in the end she couldn't. And now you've decided to shut yourself off. I didn't know her, but somehow I doubt that's what she would have wanted for you. For anybody."

His head dropped to his chest.

I realized I was holding my breath. I didn't have the right to say these things to him. He should tell me to mind my own business.

Instead, he took my hand as if I'd offered to help pull him out of a pool of water. But he still looked down. "You're right. It's not fair to her. I hadn't thought of it that way at all. She did try to stay with me. She was so strong, right to the end."

I put my hand over his, sandwiching it in my own. "And it's good that you want to honor her. But do it the way *she* would have wanted."

He looked up at me with the beginnings of a smile. "She would have liked you, just for saying that. Making me see that I've been selfish."

"Not selfish, really. But you've been hurting yourself more than she would have wanted."

He sniffed, as if he'd been holding back tears. "I pray about it constantly, but it's not something I can get over just like that."

"No one expects you to."

"I'm sorry." He struggled to regain his usual controlled expression but then, with another sniff, seemed to give up the effort. His smile was lopsided. "You probably didn't want to spend the evening talking about another woman."

"Why not?" I smiled as I realized this was payback. "We spent our first date talking about another man, remember? My ex. And you made me cry. So I think this is only fair."

He smile grew even more lopsided. Part of him wanted to laugh with me. Part of him wasn't ready yet.

I let the smile fade from my face. "I wish I had known her. She must have been an extraordinary woman. To inspire such loyalty in you even after she's gone. . ." I shook my head. "My husband didn't have much loyalty left for me while we were still living in the same house."

"Aw, now." He tried to laugh. "I don't want you comparing me with him."

"Fair enough." I looked right into his eyes. "As long as you don't compare me to her." *That's a test I will never pass, and I don't even want to try.*

He nodded.

The wet, bedraggled dog scratched at the glass door. I considered letting her in, but she was likely to growl at Brian as if she'd caught him trying to steal the silver. A cold sense of sadness descended over me as I realized she probably never would get used to having him in the house. Before too long, I might not be seeing Brian anymore. Soon he would find out that I wasn't really interested in history like Chloe had been. I just came to the site to do a job. He might even feel I'd used him to get the truth.

Which I still didn't have.

The breeze coming through the window made me shiver. "It's getting late."

"Your dog wants in."

I shrugged. "We all want things we can't have. If I spent my life trying to please the dog, the house would be wallpapered in rawhide and I would be working in a butcher's shop to get the employee discount on steaks."

He laughed for a moment, and then when his face had settled into a gentle smile, he asked, "Where do you work? I've never asked."

"Oh, I, uh. . ." Why hadn't I thought up a convenient lie? I should have been prepared for this weeks ago. "Uh, I've never asked where you work, either." *There. Throw the ball back in his court.*

"I'm a structural engineer. At URS Corp."

"URS? Is that related to the guys who drive brown trucks and wear shorts to deliver packages in winter?"

He laughed, and just like that, we were back on safe subjects. Light banter, jokes. It was easy to talk again. Jeff pulled up with the kids just as Brian was leaving, so there was no time for an awkward moment of wondering whether I should give him a hug.

It was only later that I thought of that, when the kids were in bed and I felt the cold breeze on my arms again. I wanted to hug him. I felt we had grown closer in just the short time we were together tonight. Yet I also felt time was ticking rapidly toward the moment of revelation, when he would find out how I had deceived him. And then that closeness would be gone.

I shut the window, but the chill remained in the house.

## 18

I went back to the computer and stared at it for a while without sitting down. I should keep searching now. Tomorrow would be busy in the office; I had to teach Brittany how to use new software for invoices, and auditors were coming in the afternoon to go over third quarter accounts, so I wouldn't have much time for research.

But I was tired and getting nowhere. Even though I had time now, I had no thought left in me. Maybe Athena was just the name of a cat after all. Maybe Patty had always wanted a cat and fantasized that if she got a cat she'd name it Athena and she was embarrassed that I found—

I stopped myself. *Athena.* That was the name on the paper. I could even see it now. Patty had needed to remember the name Athena. Could it be a company that she'd sold the notes to?

Yanking out the computer chair, I plopped down in it without looking, missing at least half the seat and almost ending up on the floor. I shoved the mouse around to erase the dancing dinosaur screensaver.

"Athena," I said, typing the word into the search engine. "Artifact."

Athena Analysis came up as the fourth choice. The company's Web site said they offered a wide array of techniques to analyze artifacts. So it didn't look as though she would have sold the notes to Athena, but maybe she sent them there for analysis.

The techniques they offered included radiocarbon dating, which required destruction of part of the item being tested. Mrs. McGregor and the others would never allow the notes to be harmed, so they wouldn't willingly send them off to be tested even though the tester could use a piece so small its absence would not be noticed. And they wouldn't approve the expense. But Patty wanted them tested. Could she have sent them off on her own?

How would she pay for it? She was retired, a former high school home economics teacher who probably donated every spare penny to historical sites.

She wasn't exactly the type to rob a bank.

But how about a bake sale? If she knew the money was going to help the site, she could justify it to herself. It had been her suggestion to ask John to help with the bake sale and raffle. She knew he would be blamed when the money was missing.

I threw my hands up in the air and spun the chair around in a circle. This was it! This had to be it. Patty stole the raffle money to help pay for analysis of the notes when she found out she couldn't afford it on her own.

I made the case! I spun the chair around again, kicking out my heels and knocking over the trash can, spraying pencil shavings in a wide arc across the matted carpet.

I didn't care. I made the case all on my own! I would call Athena tomorrow for confirmation, and then I could type the whole thing up and hand it to Dave when he walked in. I was ready to close my first case. He would have to give me others. Maybe we could afford to send Brittany to classes to learn the office software on her own.

If I had the paperwork with me, I could start typing up the report right now. Instead, I spun the chair around a few more times and then decided to go to bed so I could get an early start in the morning.

To get into the office earlier than usual, I dropped Evan off at his friend Nathan's house with a bag of Corn Flakes, an apple, and a plastic spork. "Sorry I forgot your drink," I apologized as I practically pushed him out of the van. "See you after school."

He gave me a cross-eyed frown but then smiled. "It's okay."

I wished I could give him a good-bye kiss right where his hair was sticking up on the top of his head, but we were practically in public. So I just watched him jog up to Nathan's front porch, ring the bell, and disappear inside.

Then it was time to switch from sentimental mom to superefficient employee. I ran yellow lights, swerved around trucks, and pressed my luck at the speed trap at the bottom of the hill, going twenty-eight in a twenty-five-mile-per-hour zone to get to the office in record time. Inside, I unlocked doors and turned on the lights, computers, copier, and other equipment with dizzying speed. I tried to call Athena Analysis, but their switchboard didn't open until nine. So I went ahead and started my report instead, knowing Dave would not get in until at least 9:30, and I still had time to get confirmation from Athena and hand him the completed report just as I'd envisioned.

At five seconds after nine, I called Athena again. I had to talk to three different people and wait on hold through about seven recorded messages, but I expected that.

What I didn't expect was the answer. Or rather, the lack of an answer. The company's confidentiality agreements prevented them from revealing whether they had received anything from Patty or anything from the 1776 House or even anything purporting to have been touched by George Washington.

They wouldn't tell me a thing without a court order.

I kicked my trash can over, knowing it was empty so I wouldn't have a mess to clean up. The visit from the DAP was in less than a week. By the time we got an order, had it served on Athena, and waited for them to return the notes, it would be too late.

The trash can spun out of control as the front door opened into it.

"What's going on?" Brittany asked, with good reason for once.

I grabbed my purse and the local phone book. "You're going to learn the accounting software on your own. I've got to go out this morning. If the auditors arrive before I get back, fix them some coffee and get them set up at the conference table."

Her anxious gaze swept over the empty coffeepot and the blank conference table. "But where are the files?"

"The file drawers are labeled, and I believe both

you and the auditors can read." I glanced at my watch. "And you have three hours to figure out how to make coffee. Good luck."

"Where are you going?"

"To catch a thief."

I had fun saying that. And the rush of adrenaline carried me out to the car and down the street to the first "Lowell" address I checked in the phone book. The house was a nondescript red brick with white siding, outlined with the usual evergreen hedges. No one answered my knock. I could see no name listed anywhere, and the mailbox was empty, so I couldn't check the occupant's identity that way. The rush of adrenaline ebbed away.

Since Patty was retired, I hoped she'd be home this morning. But now reality was catching up. Just because she was retired didn't mean she'd be sitting home waiting for me. And she might not be listed in the phone book. There were only three "Lowells."

It took me longer to get to the next house, and the assortment of bikes on the porch and the swing set in the yard told me this probably wasn't it. The last address was an apartment, and since Patty had mentioned something about her house being near Paula's, I didn't think this was it, either.

I decided to go back to the first house. My driving was well within the speed limit now; I was in no rush to find that I'd made a mistake. At the end of the street, a mail truck pulled up and parked just after I did. This was it, then. I would wait for the mail and check the name. But the mail carrier didn't emerge from the truck for so long that I began to wonder if he'd been smothered under a pile of junk flyers.

At last he came out and started to amble down the side of the street opposite the house I was watching. This was going to take awhile.

But it would work, I told myself. I would find Patty. And then—

Well, I actually hadn't considered what I would do when I found her. If I were a brilliant investigator, I would trick her into revealing her guilt. But I wasn't a brilliant anything and had proven myself to be a mediocre investigator at best.

What was I going to do? Suddenly the mail carrier seemed to be moving way too fast.

If I didn't think I could trick her, I could threaten her with jail. I pictured myself interrogating her in a bleak room like the police detectives use on TV, painting a picture of the horrible future awaiting her in prison while she sat quivering in her chair and her attorney mumbled ineffectually about reasonable doubt.

Okay, that wasn't going to happen either. I doubted that Patty had an interrogation room or a lawyer in her house. And she was too nice for me to threaten her with anything. She was almost like a friend.

If I thought a friend had done something wrong, what would I do?

When I thought Linda was having an affair with my husband, I was afraid to do anything. I waited until it was so obvious that I looked like a fool. And then I let her make excuses so she could continue to justify herself, as if I were the one at fault.

This time I would not wait. I would question Patty in the same quiet, direct way Brian had asked me about my past. Asking as someone who cared about her, not as someone just out to pry.

It worked because Brian did care about me. And I cared about Patty.

The mailman stepped into his truck and drove around the corner. A rush of leaves swirled in the truck's wake. A bird swooped across the street to land on a porch railing. But nothing else moved.

It was time to check the mail.

I cracked open the door and squeezed myself out, ducking down so I wouldn't be seen by anyone on the other side of the van. Still crouching, I tiptoed around the van, and then, after looking both ways to see if anyone other than the bird was watching me, I made a mad dash for the porch and threw myself behind an azalea bush, landing hard on my right knee.

Only then did I realize that if anyone actually was watching, my behavior would look highly suspicious, if not outright ridiculous.

The mailbox was a black metal contraption hung next to the door. I opened the lid, fished out the contents, and scanned the letters quickly. *Mrs. Lowell; P. Lowell, Resident; Homeowner Paula J. Lowell; Ms. Paula Lowell.*

This was Paula's house, not Patty's.

I stuffed the mail back into the box and dropped down behind the azalea again.

Okay, no need to give up now. Patty lived nearby. I would just have to check the mail of the houses in the immediate vicinity. As long as my knees held out, that is.

At the house next door, I banged my left knee

into a post as I tried to hide behind it. The house next to that one had a thorny bush guarding the mailbox. There had to be a better way.

Patty's house would have a nice vegetable and herb garden in back, because on Saturdays she brought in potatoes and cabbage and kale from her garden. I slipped around the house to the backyard, and from there I could see several other yards, as well. Two houses down was a fenced-in garden with beanpoles at the back. Patty's garden.

I took a deep breath and marched calmly back out into the front yard and down to Patty's house. My knees were shaking as I mounted the porch steps, but this could have been just their reaction to the sight of another porch.

I rang the doorbell without stopping to check the mailbox. If this wasn't Patty's house, I would simply tell whoever answered that I was selling Avon.

"Why, Karen, this is a surprise." Patty's face beamed through the screen door. There was a *click* as she unlatched the door then held it open.

Despite the smile, I started to feel a little uneasy. I wondered if I should have waited for Dave. Confronting the suspect alone might not have been such a great idea after all.

"What brings you here?" she asked cheerfully.

I noticed a small paring knife in her left hand. Since she was wearing an apron, my first assumption was that she had simply been in the act of cutting something up when I rang the bell. I never felt I had anything to fear from Patty, since I thought she liked me.

But I also thought she wasn't the type to steal money,

and yet now I was going to accuse her of just that.

Dave's voice echoed in my head. *"Some of the best actors in the world never set foot on the stage."*

Could she be only pretending she was pleased to see me? Just to be safe, I stepped in to stand on her right side, away from the knife. "I, uh, need to talk to you about something."

"Well, we'd better get comfortable, then. Come in here." She beckoned toward a sofa in the living room. Light from the tall windows illuminated immense bookcases that dwarfed the other furniture in the room. "Is it about Brian?" she called over her shoulder with a grin as she slipped the knife into the pocket of her apron.

I waited until she sat down, and then I took a seat close to her, but not too close.

"Um, no." I looked her straight in the eye. "It's about you."

"Oh, okay." She laughed. "Well, go ahead, then." She seemed to find my serious expression very funny.

I looked down at the antique tea table in front of us.

"Would you like something to drink?" Patty started to get up. "And I've got some really good scones from—"

I held up my hand to interrupt. "Please, just stay here for a minute." My mouth went dry as she sat back down, the smile fading from her face. But she didn't look uneasy or fearful. She looked as though she was concerned more for me than for herself.

I trusted my instinct then—I had no need to fear that she would try to hurt me. But I did fear that if I was wrong, I would not only fail to make the case and embarrass myself, I would embarrass or offend her.

I looked at the tea table again. Then I forced myself to face her. "Athena Analysis. Did you send the Washington notes there to be analyzed?"

She blinked. "Why would you. . ." Her words trailed off as she stared at me.

I tried to clear my throat, but my voice came out as a dry squeak anyway. "And you used the money from the bake sale to pay for the analysis? It was for the good of the site," I added quickly. "If the notes were proven authentic, then everyone would benefit."

After a moment in which she simply stared at me, she finally nodded, looking down at the tea table just as I had a moment ago. Her shoulders slumped as she let out a long sigh, making her seem to grow smaller. "Every time I proposed that we have them tested, no one agreed. Paula insisted it was a waste of money." She looked up at me with a grim smile. "I frankly think she didn't want to be proven wrong. And of course Eileen and Ann didn't want the notes harmed in any way. I think they thought the researchers would dissolve the leather or cut it to shreds or something. All they needed was a tiny fragment for the tests. It was worth it, really."

"Was it?" I asked softly. "An innocent man is accused of theft. Everyone assumes John Holbrock stole money from the site. The trustees who had their hopes pinned on publicity from the DAP visit have lost the site's claim to fame. Six years they waited for this visit. And now the time comes and they have only an empty case to display."

"But the site has so much more to offer," Patty insisted.

"The site has a great deal to offer those who are already drawn to history," I clarified. "But what is the attraction for the average person? George Washington slept there. They want to be where he was. And when they come, then they see all the other things the site has to offer. But without him, most people will never set foot through the door. This visit from the DAP is the chance to show everyone in the area that they can come to the 1776 House and be touched by greatness. Do you want to take away that chance?"

She looked away again. "No."

I took a deep breath. "Will you call Athena and ask them to return the notes by overnight delivery?"

Her mouth moved for some moments before any sound came out. "B–but the testing is not finished. It won't be finished for weeks."

"Will you call anyway?"

She made no answer.

"This was not your decision to make," I added softly.

A tear squeezed out of the corner of her eye and ran down her cheek. "No one else would make the decision. No one else understood. I think you do. Just as you said, everyone would benefit. But you're asking me to stop the testing now, when we're so close to learning the truth."

I nodded. "I'm asking you to stop the testing. The tests might well prove inconclusive. And the chance at the publicity, at the credibility of the DAP's visit, will be gone."

She was shaking her head, her gaze cast down and her arms crossed in front of her chest.

I leaned down to catch her gaze. "You had no right

to take the notes. And you have no right to keep them away."

She pressed her lips together so tightly they formed a hard white line. Then she nodded once, a barely perceptible motion of the head. "But you know it was the right thing to do," she said hoarsely. "I had to try."

"And if the timing were different, maybe the trustees would allow the notes to remain away awhile longer. But right now, they want them back in the case."

"Very well." She let out a sigh that came out through her nose like a snort. "I'll get them back."

"A—and there's more." I wasn't sure if I should press my luck now or try to involve the police, or at least Dave. "You'll need to repay the money."

"I know," she said morosely. "It will take time."

"You'll have to work out arrangements with the trustees. And you'll need to tell everyone. You need to clear John's name. It's not fair to him."

"Yes, yes, I realize that," she said, growing annoyed as if I were her mother reminding her that she needed to clean her room. "Can I give Athena one more day? If they send the notes back tomorrow, the house will have them by Monday."

"Call them now. The exhibit needs to be back in position as soon as possible."

She nodded in resignation, and I watched her rise and walk slowly over to a writing desk in the corner. She fumbled around for the number, dialed, and made her request.

The case was over. I had won.

## 19

I should have felt triumphant on Saturday when I stepped out of the van and heard the gravel crunch under my feet in the parking lot of the 1776 House. Patty was ready to confess, and I could announce to Mrs. McGregor that the notes would be back in her hands Monday morning.

And then I would never see the place again.

I had told Patty that I worked for an investigation firm; by now she had surely told Paula and probably everyone else, including Brian. When they found out I wasn't a real volunteer, no one would want to talk to me.

But Ann, at least, was happy to see me. She rushed up and gave me a little hug as I entered the gift shop. "Eileen says the notes will be returned Monday, and we have you to thank for it."

"So she knows already?"

She nodded several times. "Oh yes. Patty confessed the whole despicable business on the phone last night."

"Oh. Good." So much for my moment of triumph. There really was no reason for me to be here, then. Except to say good-bye.

Ann fluttered away. "Well, I'd better get going. I have to wash all the glass shelves and I've hardly started."

I didn't offer to help. "Good luck."

As I stepped out into the yard, I was nearly flattened by a large tabletop that John and Brian were carrying over to the shaded area where John held his carpentry demonstrations.

Neither of them gave any sign that they had even seen me, and I was afraid to say anything. After all, being ignored was not quite the same thing as being shunned.

Paula was wiping windows with a rag, and she didn't say anything to me either.

I glanced at the place on my wrist where my watch would be if I weren't dressed in eighteenth-century clothes. Evan had a soccer game in about half an hour. I usually didn't go to his games on weekends when he was with his dad, but this time, I thought that I should.

I didn't belong at the 1776 House anymore.

⁓

On Monday, while I undid the mistakes Brittany made in the invoices, I thought about the House and the upcoming visit of the DAP. I should have stayed to help the others finish their last-minute preparations. Brian didn't call to ask why I hadn't been there, so I assumed he really had seen me and had deliberately chosen not to speak with me.

On Tuesday while I raced to the overnight drop box, I thought of the preliminary visit of the DAP site coordinator. Could she see clearly through the windows? Did she like the smoke stains in the kitchen?

On Wednesday I accomplished virtually nothing because I was imagining the scene at the house, the volunteers demonstrating their crafts, Mrs. McGregor beaming as she proudly displayed the Washington notes in their case, cameras flashing as reporters took down every detail. I hoped they got some good pictures of Brian at the forge, even if he refused to call me.

On Thursday there was a short article about the 1776 House in the local paper, with a picture of DAP president Lucinda Fotheringill smiling in front of an American flag. She could have been standing in front of the courthouse, or library, or any public building for that matter. No picture of Brian.

On Friday afternoon, just as I was about to leave, Dave called me into his office. "It's been such a busy week!" He leaned back in his chair and stuffed a handful of cheese crackers into his mouth.

To me the week had been slow and dull, and I was anxious to end it. So I said nothing that might encourage him to prolong my visit to his office.

"I 'aven't 'ad a 'ance to really talk to you about the mffgurgurkess." He wiped his hands on the arms of his desk chair.

"I beg your pardon?"

He swallowed. "The McGregor case. I never talked to you about it."

"I gave you the final report."

"Yeah, I know. But I wanted to tell you what a good job you did. You really hit the nail on the head with that Lowell woman."

I shrugged, but secretly I was thrilled with his compliment. "Mrs. McGregor suspected her and her sister right from the start."

"Yeah, but it wasn't logical. Glad you figured it out."

"Thank you."

"And since you did such a good job," Dave continued, dumping another handful of crackers into his hand, "I thought I might offer you the lead on another case." He shoved the crackers into his mouth, but there were too many even for that oversized orifice, and some of them fell onto the floor instead. He rolled his chair back away from the desk, grinding the crackers into the wood.

I pointed toward the mess. "I'm not cleaning that up."

He shrugged. "The cleaning people will get 'em."

"They don't come until next Friday."

"Brittany can—"

"Brittany will be busy with typing lessons." I marched back into the main part of the office, pulled the portable vacuum from its perch on the wall, and tossed it to Dave. "Don't forget to put it back when you're done."

"Do you want to hear about this case or not?"

"I'm not sure I want to do this every Saturday if I'm not getting paid."

"Okay." He waved his box of crackers in frustration. "I'll pay you for any Saturdays. Deal?"

I took the box and poured myself a handful. "Shoot."

"It's the Blue Moon Gallery on Main Street. They've got a problem with damaged merchandise. We're so close to Main Street, I thought you could look into this without too much trouble. Are you willing?"

I tried not to look too gleeful. "Sure, why not?" I shoved crackers into my mouth just as he had done, dropping three of them. I was going to leave them on the floor, but I just couldn't. I reached down to pick them up.

"Doing anything fun this weekend?" he asked, *before* he stuffed the crackers into his mouth this time.

I shrugged. "Soccer game first thing Saturday, but no drama practice. Maybe we'll go see a movie." Because we didn't have to go to the 1776 House in the afternoon.

Weekends would be less hectic now. This was a good thing. And if I missed the friends I had made at the site, I had learned that I could make friends, and that was the important thing. At least, I kept telling myself that.

"Have fun!" Dave waved after me as I headed out to begin my weekend.

The morning had only just started to warm by the time Evan's soccer game ended. I tossed my empty paper coffee cup in the trash before heading over to congratulate him.

"That was the last game of the regular season, right?"

He nodded, his mouth full of bright orange Cheetos.

"Congratulations!" I knew better than to hug him in public, but I gave him a quick squeeze anyway.

"We didn't win." He shook his head in disgust and then drowned his sorrows with a big swig of Gatorade. "It was a tie."

"You didn't lose. Nobody lost. A happy ending, in my book. So where should we go to celebrate?" I was hoping for someplace with good coffee and nothing orange, because I figured Evan already had enough food-coloring stains on his face to last the rest of the weekend.

Alicia prodded me on the shoulder. "We don't have time to go out."

"We have to get to the House, don't we?" Evan asked.

"It opened an hour ago." Alicia glared down her nose at me. "And we're not even dressed yet."

I couldn't believe I had forgotten to tell them. I guess I had been saving it for a surprise. Just when they were complaining about having to go, I would tell them they didn't have to after all.

Except that they hadn't complained this weekend. Either of them.

"You know, guys," I began, "we don't have to go every Saturday. In fact, we don't have to go anymore at all."

"D'ya mean we've learned all the history we need to know?" Evan asked hopefully. "Forever?"

I cringed. "Er, no."

"It means," Alicia cut in, "that Mom broke up with her boyfriend, and she doesn't want to go there and see him again."

"He's not my boyfriend," I hissed. I didn't think she had even seen Brian and me together. "I don't even know who you mean."

"You do know." She giggled. "The blacksmith guy. The one with all the muscles."

I rolled my eyes. "We did not break up. We were never really going out."

Evan looked at me with an unusually serious expression. "You have a boyfriend?"

I was hissing again. "We are not going to discuss this here in the middle of the soccer field!"

Evan looked at the grass. "We're on the edge, actually."

"Let's go for donuts." I grabbed his arm to pull him toward the car.

Alicia crossed her arms in front of her chest. "Since I don't have practice today, I want to go to the House. I haven't even said good-bye to Patty. If you don't want to see *him*, you can stay in the car."

I turned to Evan. "Is that okay with you? Is it okay if we go say good-bye?"

"Sure." He shrugged. "That's where I figured we were going anyway."

"Fine. Let's go, then." I would show Alicia I wasn't trying to avoid Brian at all. But given his reaction to me last Saturday, I suppose I wasn't all that anxious to see him, either.

Maybe I *would* wait in the car.

I was not that great a coward, as it turned out. I decided I would apologize to any of the volunteers who felt deceived by my presence the last few weeks, including *him*.

Although Alicia and Evan headed around the side of the house directly for the outbuildings, I decided to start in the house with Ann and Mrs. McGregor, who had no reason to hate me. I was still a little bit of a coward.

But it was Paula I found talking with Ann in the gift shop. Both of them were leaning over a manila folder filled with eight-by-ten photos.

"It's a shame Brian isn't in any of these shots," Paula mused. "A good photo of him at the forge with his shirtsleeves rolled up, and we'd likely double our attendance among female visitors."

Ann nodded.

Then they heard me enter.

"Karen!" Paula's face split into an uncharacteristic smile. "How are you feeling? We heard you went home sick last week."

"I—I'm fine."

"Come look at the pictures from the DAP photographer." She held up the folder. "He got some great shots."

"You said Brian wasn't in them?"

"He was out of town on business all week." Her forehead split with frown lines. "He may still be out. I can't remember."

"Oh." That explained why he hadn't called me all week.

It didn't explain why I hadn't tried to call him. If I thought he was angry at me, I could have tried to apologize or at least explain. But instead, I realized I'd been waiting for him to call me.

I was waiting for him to prove that he cared, and I was letting him fail a test he didn't even know he was taking.

"I'm going to go see where the kids have gone," I murmured as I headed for the door into the yard. Evan would naturally go to the blacksmith shop, so I'd "look" for him first.

But when I stepped out into the yard, my attention

was diverted by a cluster of people near the springhouse. Mrs. McGregor stood at the center of the group, holding a manila folder like the one Ann and Paula examined in the gift shop. Patty, John, and another woman gathered close, leaning over the folder.

"More pictures?" I asked.

Mrs. McGregor shook her head. "This is the proof of the article that will accompany the pictures."

"I did not say that," John objected suddenly. "I did not say that the wild cherry tree in the yard is from the same stock as the one chopped down by George Washington."

I stepped over to join them. "Did they mention anything about the authentic smoke stains?"

Patty laughed. "Not so far."

Mrs. McGregor turned a withering gaze on her. "I still cannot believe that you went to so much trouble to dirty up the walls we had just whitewashed."

Patty narrowed her eyes at her. "I want my kitchen to look authentic, not pretty."

"It's not your kitchen."

"Can I, um, see that page?" I hoped to distract the women from their escalating conflict.

Patty ignored me as she glared at Mrs. McGregor. "I conceded you the house. I gave you back your precious notes, and you'll have your money back soon, with interest. But the kitchen *is* mine because you don't care about it."

Mrs. McGregor looked as if she was about to object. Then she shut her mouth.

They both went back to reading.

I couldn't really focus on the words. Instead, I was

listening to the clang of a hammer on the anvil coming from the blacksmith shop. Brian was definitely back, and I wanted to talk to him. "I'll wait until it's not so crowded." I smiled and stepped back from the group.

John came over to join me. "Thank you," he said in a low voice. "I hear you're the private investigator they hired to find the Washington notes, and you got Patty to confess that she stole the notes and the money. She made sure everyone knew I had nothing to do with it."

I blushed. "Well, I'm not really a. . ." I stopped. I *was* an investigator. And I was entitled to credit for solving the case. "I'm glad I could help. So how did the DAP visit go?"

He frowned. "Well enough, except the reporter was apparently unable to quote people with anything approaching accuracy."

"Did they like the Washington notes?"

"Didn't pay much attention to 'em, actually. The House Committee decided to put the case in a corner so they're not so obvious anymore."

"Was anything said about test results?"

"The leather and ink are approximately the right age, but there's a lot of room for error. They didn't have time to do the handwriting analysis, so we don't know whether ol' George really wrote the milk punch recipe or not."

I stared at him. "That's what the notes were about?"

"Yeah. You didn't know?"

"Nope. All this fuss over a recipe?" I shook my head incredulously. Then I looked at John. "So now your name is clear, but what about Patty? What are they going to do to her?"

He shrugged. "She promised to pay back the bake sale money and the money paid to your investigation agency, but she didn't offer to resign from the board, and they didn't ask her to, as far as I know. She had to listen to an earful from Eileen McGregor, and she'll probably get reminded at every meeting." He grinned. "And that's punishment enough for anybody."

I was inclined to agree.

"Uh-oh!" He ran to protect his carpentry tools from a herd of Cub Scouts that thundered out of the house and across the yard.

If I was going to talk to Brian, I would have to get to him before they did.

Brian was working with Evan as I walked in, holding a piece of iron with tongs while Evan hammered the red-hot end against the anvil.

"Mom, watch this! I'm making a rat tail." He hammered several more times, making no discernable impression in the metal whatsoever.

"Whoa, whoa, stop now," Brian cautioned gently. "It's getting too cool; it could crack." He flashed me a brief smile before turning to lay the metal back on the glowing coals.

I stood sort of helplessly, unsure what to say. I wanted to talk to Brian about so many things, and yet this was obviously the wrong time and place. He was in his element, demonstrating a craft he loved. It would be unfair to draw him away right now.

Brian pushed the metal to the side. "Evan, guard the forge for a minute. I want to have a word with your mom." He turned to me. "Do you mind? It won't take long."

"Mind?" I shook my head and followed him out a side door to a covered enclosure for storing coal. It was a dark, dank place that smelled of oily rock.

"Hey," he said in a low voice, his voice echoing softly off the wooden walls. "I just wanted to say I'm sorry I didn't call this week to see how you were doing. I didn't hear you were sick until this morning."

I grimaced. "I'm not sick."

"Well, I mean last week. I got called to California to troubleshoot a project—just got back last night."

"I wasn't sick last week either."

"You weren't?" His brow wrinkled in confusion. "But you looked so pale when I saw you, and then you left so suddenly, I should have realized. . .but someone said today you had been sick."

"I looked pale?" I thought he hadn't even seen me.

"Well, I just caught a quick glimpse while I was helping John with the tabletop. And then you were gone."

"I thought you were all mad at me," I mumbled, suddenly ashamed to realize how self-centered I'd been. They weren't thinking of me at all. They were just working.

He put a hand on my arm. "Why should we be mad at you?"

"Well. . ." I started to look away but then made myself focus on his face. "Because I wasn't really honest. I didn't tell you I was here to investigate the theft."

He grinned, his teeth glowing white in the darkness. "Well, you couldn't exactly do that, could you?"

"And you're not mad? You're not mad that I was pretending to. . ." I let the words trail off. I was going to say, "pretending to be interested in history," but I wasn't really pretending. I actually did find some of it interesting.

"Pretending to work hard? You did that pretty convincingly as far as I could see."

"Pretending to be something I'm not," I said at last. "All this," I confessed, waving toward the petticoats, "isn't really me. I like to wear jeans."

"Well, so do I, most of the time."

"And I don't really want to spend every Saturday here washing diapers in the yard."

"I wouldn't want to, either. I come here to practice an art that I enjoy. I can't imagine that anyone enjoys laundry."

"Paula seems to."

He glanced toward the yard. "I think she likes the idea of demonstrating past skills. But the reality is backbreaking labor. I think she'd rather talk about it than do it. And let the kids try it out."

"I hadn't thought of that." I should have let the visiting kids do the work while I talked.

"So maybe you'll come back sometime?" He had a hopeful gleam in his eye that was impossible to disappoint.

"Yeah, when I can." *And will that be the only time I see you?* I was afraid to ask.

He grew suddenly shy, or else he found his shoes suddenly fascinating. "Hey, um, the kids asked about you on Sunday."

"The kids?"

"My youth group. Jesse and the others."

I nodded. "Oh yeah." The waiters at the dinner.

They had so much fun I still had trouble thinking of it as a church. "So what did they ask?"

"They asked if they were going to see you again."

I licked my lips nervously. "And what did you say?"

"I said it was up to you." That hopeful gleam in his eyes was still there.

I started to get hopeful, too, until I realized that he wasn't exactly asking me out again; he was asking me to go to church. "I'm not really a church person," I admitted.

"Well, I was hoping you might consider helping me out. We'll be starting rehearsals for the Christmas play in a week or two, and I need an assistant director."

"Do you want Alicia?"

He shook his head. "Alicia can help. But my *assistant* will have to stay close to me, consult on the production, help revise the script—I think there will be a lot of extra meetings. Outside the church. Probably some meetings over dinner. . ."

He couldn't just ask me out. He had to give it a reason. And that was okay—probably his way of dealing with Chloe-guilt. I was good with that, for now anyway.

This wasn't good-bye at all.

"So can you help me?" He finished with a disarming smile.

But I wasn't ready to be completely disarmed by a man again just yet. "I get to wear normal clothes, right? No goofy caps?"

"That cap looks cute on you." He leaned closer. "But no, you don't have to wear it."

He wasn't going to turn me into a history nut. But

he might end up turning me into a church person, despite what I'd said earlier. There was a sense of fun and camaraderie in his church that had long been missing in my life. I knew that church was supposed to make you feel closer to God, but I had always found it so boring that I wasn't even sure I wanted to *be* close to God. But now, from what I'd observed in Brian, I was starting to think that maybe God didn't require us to be bored in order to get close to Him. I guess I could give church another try.

I still had one more point to insist on. "I'll have to miss rehearsal if it conflicts with my job." I had another case to work on, and that would take priority over amateur theatricals.

He clasped my arm in his. "Just don't miss the extra dinner meetings too often. You know, just like you said, 'You've got to eat, even if you're busy.' "

I blinked. "You remember that?"

He chuckled. "It was the first time a woman asked me out in about fifteen years. Yeah, I remember. I was scared to pieces."

"I was, too." I laid my head against his shoulder. "It was the first time I asked anyone out, ever. Or at least the first time that it mattered."

I think Brian just might have kissed me right there in the dark, dank coal shed if Evan hadn't stuck his head around the corner at that moment.

"Cub Scouts!" he yelped. "About a million of them."

"I'm there," Brian called back. He brushed a kiss against my hand as he headed back into the shop. "We'd better get busy on the script right away. I have a feeling it's going to need a lot of changes."

I smiled. "Change is a good thing." My hand had this nice tingling feeling, and I knew that this was only the beginning.

Like her heroine, K. D. is a "soccer mom" living in an old town that has become a suburb of Baltimore. But unlike her heroine, she is still happily married, active in her church, and visits every historical site she can manage. It took her almost thirty-five years to realize that she had always wanted to be a writer. During those years, she worked at a variety of different jobs, serving as everything from a bookkeeper and preschool teaching assistant to a newspaper columnist, hostess in a hospitality suite at NASCAR races, and corporate attorney for a pest control company. She reports that being a mom is the best job of all, but that writing books runs a close second.

You may correspond with this author by writing:
K. D. Hays
Author Relations
PO Box 721
Uhrichsville, OH 44683

# A Letter to Our Readers

Dear Reader:

In order to help us satisfy your quest for more great mystery stories, we would appreciate it if you would take a few minutes to respond to the following questions. We welcome your comments and read each form and letter we receive. When completed, please return to:

Fiction Editor
**Heartsong Presents—MYSTERIES!**
PO Box 721
Uhrichsville, Ohio 44683

Did you enjoy reading *George Washington Stepped Here* by K. D. Hays?

Very much! I would like to see more books like this! The one thing I particularly enjoyed about this story was:

_____

_____

_____

Moderately. I would have enjoyed it more if:

_____

_____

_____

Are you a member of the HP—MYSTERIES! Book Club?
Yes    No

If no, where did you purchase this book?

_____

Please rate the following elements using a scale of 1 (poor) to 10 (superior):

___ Main character/sleuth          ___ Romance elements

___ Inspirational theme            ___ Secondary characters

___ Setting                        ___ Mystery plot

How would you rate the cover design on a scale of 1 (poor) to 5 (superior)?_____

What themes/settings would you like to see in future **Heartsong Presents—MYSTERIES!** selections? _____
_____
_____

Please check your age range:
  ◯ Under 18      ◯ 18–24
  ◯ 25–34         ◯ 35–45
  ◯ 46–55         ◯ Over 55

Name: _____

Occupation: _____

Address: _____

E-mail address: _____

# Heartsong Presents

## Great Mysteries at a Great Price! Purchase Any Title for Only $4.97 Each!

## HEARTSONG PRESENTS— MYSTERIES! TITLES AVAILABLE NOW:

# MYSTERIES!

*Heartsong Presents—MYSTERIES!* provide romance and faith interwoven among the pages of these fun whodunits. Written by the talented and brightest authors in this genre, such as Christine Lynxwiler, Cecil Murphey, Nancy Mehl, Dana Mentink, Candice Speare, and many others, these cozy tales are sure to challenge your mind, warm your heart, touch your spirit—and put your sleuthing skills to the test.

*Not all titles may be available at time of order.*
If outside the U.S., please call
740-922-7280 for shipping charges.

# A BRIDE SO FAIR

Emily Ralston is delighted when she lands a job at the Children's Building at the World's Fair. When a lost boy is found by a handsome guard and soon after a dead body turns up, the mystery begins to unfold. Can Emily deliver little Adam to safety before time runs out?

ISBN 978-59789-492-0
288 pages, $10.97

# OHIO
# *Weddings*

## 3 stories in 1

Secrets, love, and danger are afoot when three remarkable women reexamine their lives on Bay Island. Lauren Wright returns to straighten out her past only to disrupt her future. Becky Merrill steps onto the shore and into sabotage. Judi Rydell can't outrun her former life. Who will rescue their hearts?

ISBN 978-1-59789-987-1
Contemporary, paperback, 352 pages

# Beloved Castaway

Isabelle Gayarre is desperate for her freedom. Captain Josiah Carter is her only way out. Together they may lose their lives and their hearts. Can this runaway slave and godless sea captain find the fair haven they so desperately seek? Or will they be torn apart upon the stormy seas off the Florida Keys?

ISBN 978-1-59789-593-4, $10.97